The Cord

THE CORD

Resource Publications
An Imprint of Wipf and Stock Publishers
199 W. 8th Ave., Suite 3
Eugene, OR 97401

www.wipfandstock.com

ISBN 13: 978-1-4982-2963-0

Manufactured in the U.S.A.   07/13/2015

Unless otherwise identified, all Scripture quotations in this publication are taken from the New American Standard Bible (NASB), © The Lockman Foundation 1960, 1962, 1963, 1968, 1971, 1972, 1973, 1975, 1977.

One Day! Hymn written by J. Wilbur Chapman in 1910. (Public Domain)

All Hail the Power of Jesus' Name! Hymn written by Edward Perronet in 1780. (Public Domain)

The Cord

Stephen W. Robbins

RESOURCE *Publications* · Eugene, Oregon

To Ruth
My flourishing companion on the Way

Acknowledgements

A WISE PERSON (ONE with a long view of the good life) advised people over fifty years old to try something completely new. For me to enter the world of fiction fulfills this midlife benchmark. Outside of long-ago classroom required reading, I can count on one hand the novels I have read. Though my pastoral calling and interests bury me deep in non-fiction, the power of story has diffused a quickening ray in the basement of libraries filled with commentaries, dictionaries, and journals.

I want to thank my family for keeping me on track and cheering me on throughout this novel adventure. Ruth, Elizabeth, and Stephen, thank you for holding my hand as I stumbled into creative writing, a land that you are at home and flourish in. At your request, I do acknowledge that all characters in this story are purely fictitious, and any resemblance is purely coincidental. (As Elizabeth avowed, "Grandma, I am *not* Anne!")

I also want to thank the Sparks family and Lori Shanebeck for their constructive encouragement, and Terri Garcia, Stephanie Townsend, Chris Acosta, and my mom (Beverly Robbins) for proofreading earlier drafts of *The Cord*. Your fresh eyes enhanced the story and saved me much embarrassment. My heartfelt gratitude goes out to Pastors Joel Fairley and Paul Langford. Your ruthless insistence that I finish the story gave me strength to write the hardest line in the book. Thank you!

1

"Beautiful sermon, Pastor."

Pastor Donovan smiled as he heard this and the other customary tributes from his parishioners as they filed out after the service. Week after week he shook their hands in the foyer as they exited through the double doors out to their cars and into their worlds. And week after week he heard the same praise. "Great sermon, Pastor." "You really gave us something to think about." "I really enjoyed your sermon." And, of course, Brother Bob's "Boy, you really hit a homerun today, Pastor."

Smiling on the outside, Pastor Donovan doubted every word. *Homerun? Really? A foul ball, maybe.* A nagging voice inside kept asking, "Is this making any difference? Do these people ever go home changed?"

"Pastor, may I speak to you when you're done here?"

"Of course," said Pastor Donovan instinctively with a smile. Immediately, though, questions bounced around in his head. *Why does this man, a visitor, want to talk? Is he going to ambush me with a theological litmus test? Does he want to volunteer to be a leader, teach a class, or sing a solo?* Ever since the infamous oboe-playing guest who punctuated the congregational worship with an impromptu concert, daunting flashbacks of visitors offering their "gifts" had caused Pastor Donovan's heart to skip beats.

When the last parishioner finally left, Pastor Donovan reassured his wife and two kids as they stood by the family car, "I'll only be a few minutes." He then walked to the man waiting and said in his best pastoral voice, "How may I help you?"

"Actually, Pastor, I want to help you."

Pastor Donovan readied himself. The well-rehearsed "oboe-player" speech bounced through his head, but he resisted dismissing the man and postured himself to listen. "Please forgive me, but I don't recall ever meeting you. What is your name?"

"My name is George Carlson. I do research at SarkiSystems. That's actually what I want to talk to you about. But before I do, may we sit down?"

"Sure," acquiesced Pastor Donovan as he gestured toward the back pew of the sanctuary.

"Before I explain how I might help you, I want to ask you: Do you ever wonder if what you are doing makes any difference? Do you ever get frustrated at how little the church impacts the world today? Would you like to see 'Thy kingdom come, Thy will be done' become a worldwide reality, not merely a weekly prayer?"

Pastor Donovan wanted to cry out a wholehearted "Amen," but he stopped himself and stared warily at the stranger whose words too closely expressed longings hidden yet growing with each passing Sunday. Guarded, Pastor Donovan answered, "Sure. Who wouldn't want to see more change?"

Placing his hand on the pastor's shoulder, George said with a smile that indicated insight, "I sense that you *really* want this. Let me just say—and I know that you have other things you need to do right now—that there have been advancements in my research that I know will intrigue you, if not revive and embolden your ministry and calling. So, if you are interested, please come to SarkiSystems tomorrow night. I will be meeting with a few others after work to discuss how technology and faith can finally, and I mean with finality, work together." With this announcement, George stood up, shook Pastor Donovan's hand, and exited the sanctuary.

Pastor Donovan sat for a moment, alone on the aging mahogany pew. "I know that you have other things you need to do right now." These words, uttered by George as an aside, stirred up both discontent and hope inside him. *What other things? What's more important than my calling?* Feeling like the withered man at the pool of Bethesda, Pastor Donovan wondered if this stirring of the water was for him this time? Was George his Jesus asking him, "Do you wish to get well?" Was the invitation to this meeting tomorrow his own "Arise, take up your pallet, and walk" moment of truth? Or would this be yet another disappointment?

* * * * *

Mondays were Pastor Donovan's day off. He usually woke up second-guessing what he said and did the day before. Regret, resentment, and self-criticism tired his body and consumed his spirit. At times, especially over this past year, he had considered making a change. For brief moments he thought about leaving the ministry. But mostly he thought about switching his day off. *Why not be the "Monday morning pastor" at the office, shuffle papers piled on the desk, make a few phone calls, go home, and then take a different day off when not so drained, so spent? Why waste days off exhausted?*

This morning was no different. Pastor Donovan got up late and read the paper as he ate breakfast. The stranger's words kept repeating themselves in his head. The man claimed to have discovered something that would "revive and embolden" his ministry. Pastor Donovan put down the paper and gazed out the window. What was SarkiSystems and how could a research lab do something for his ministry? He opened his laptop computer and stared at the screen for a few minutes before putting his fingers to the keyboard and typing in "SarkiSystems." In seconds, a screen full of selections popped up. One stood out: "SarkiSystems Takes the Lead in Genetic Research." The article relayed how SarkiSystems had recently announced advancements in the use of human umbilical cord-derived stem cells. Apparently, they successfully treated Alzheimer's patients using this therapy. Pastor Donovan sat back in his chair. How could a lab that specialized in developing disease therapies possibly help his ministry?

Thoughts of SarkiSystems and the stranger's confident assertion that he could renew Pastor Donovan's ministry nagged at him throughout the day. As his wife put a family-favorite casserole of chicken and rice in the oven for the evening meal, he looked at her and said, "That man yesterday, he said he could help with ministry."

"What's he trying to sell?"

"He's from a genetics laboratory and he didn't say anything about selling a new program or anything. I don't know. He was so confident. He said to come see him at his office tonight if I'm interested."

"Well, you know you're not going to rest until you check it out, so go. I'll record the game for you."

Two and a half hours later, he sat in the car outside SarkiSystems wondering why, on a night he typically sat inert with only enough energy to hold the TV remote, he was going to a meeting with a man he hardly knew. With a sigh, he exited the car and stared at a white-stuccoed building in an industrial area on the outskirts of town. As semi trucks passed by, only large black address numbers set the non-descript, box-shaped structure apart from the others. Dark clouds in the dusky sky reflected off the building's windows as Pastor Donovan walked toward the only opened door and lighted room.

"Good evening," said George as Pastor Donovan peeked his head through the door. "Please come in. I'm so glad you came. With you here, we can now begin the meeting."

Pastor Donovan counted three men already in the room with George Carlson, as well as four chairs set up in front of a podium. To the left of the podium stood a projector and screen; to the right stood a small table with something resting on top and wrapped in cloths.

"Men, please have a seat." With this instruction, George began the meeting. "I want to welcome you here tonight. This gathering marks the beginning of the consummation of God's unfolding plan for humanity. He is about to write history—*His story*—on the pages of our lives. But before I unveil the key, or shall I say *the cord* (I'll explain what I mean in a minute), let's introduce ourselves to one another. Arbe, let's begin with you. Tell us your name, what you do for a living, and why you are here."

"Good evening. My name, as you just heard, is Arbe. I retired a year ago from the Marines. I'm here because I want peace on earth."

"Hello. I'm Maxwell, one of George's co-workers. My reason for being here is to offer support and a second opinion when needed."

Next in line to share, Pastor Donovan cleared his throat, but not his nerves. "I'm Payne. I am a pastor in town. And, to be honest, I'm not exactly sure why I am here except that George invited me."

"It will become clearer to you in a moment," noted George as he motioned to the final gentleman to be introduced.

"I'm Dr. Greybellum. I am a professor at a seminary in Israel. My reason for being here is simple. I want to see Jesus *prosopon pros prosopon*."

What on earth did I get myself into? Pastor Donovan instantly second-guessed his decision to come as he considered the company. *"Peace on earth?"* What kind of beauty contest answer is that? And "prosopon pros prosopon?" *Really? Are we to decipher this ivory tower code, or simply be impressed? What kind of genetics lab is this?* Before he could politely excuse himself, the lights in the room dimmed. With hands over his heart, and with great eagerness in his voice, George invited the men to fix their eyes on the screen.

* * * * *

Footage of Arbe introducing his team and their mission projected onto the screen. Mr. "Peace on Earth" was dressed in fatigues, armed with weaponry fit for any covert operation. Though not studio quality, the video and audio were understandable. The operation itself, however, needed much clarification.

"We're going in now," narrated Arbe as the team entered a dark passageway. Vigilant, yet swiftly, they made their way down a corridor adorned with images and symbols carved into the walls. "Straight-ahead are stairs, leading down to the sisters." Arbe's voice beamed with anticipation. Unevenly carved out of dirt and stone and spiraling downward, the stairs slowed the team's campaign. At the bottom, roughly two stories underground, stood a wooden door, seemingly petrified over centuries, with no visible handle.

"Break it down," whispered a team member into their communication headsets.

"No," insisted Arbe. "Knock."

A collective "Knock?" transmitted from the team.

"No force, remember? Only if necessary will we use force."

Fully armed, the six men stood still, at attention, in front of the door, Arbe instructed the closest team member to knock.

He knocked three times, each one echoing in the chamber.

Nothing.

Impatient, he banged on the door.

"Stop it," said Arbe sternly. "We wait."

Pastor Donovan found himself mesmerized by images captured by body-mounted cameras. Though he remained clueless as to the what, where, and why, he leaned forward in his chair, not wanting to miss a single word or detail.

The chamber door began to open. The team members, including Arbe, readied their trigger fingers. No force. But they were prepared, if necessary.

An elderly lady greeted them with an exhaling, submissive smile. Like the door she opened, her face looked aged with purpose. She motioned for them to enter. Fingers still on triggers, the team entered, surveying the room. Candles along the walls provided sufficient lighting for the video. Seven ladies, all but one dressed in simple white robes, stood like sentries around a table in the center of the room, guarding who knows what.

Arbe approached the ladies. "Sisters, the Lord bless you and keep you. On behalf of God's people around the world and throughout the ages, we thank you for your faithfulness and diligence. You have fulfilled your duty well. The time has come, however, to relinquish the cord. The time has come for our blessed hope to materialize. The key to conquer all evil is at hand. *The* means of grace abides in the cord's blood!" Arbe stepped forward, stretched out his left hand (his right hand still battle-ready), and stated firmly, "Sisters, the time has come to release the power in the blood."

With their bare feet firmly planted on the floor, the sisters did not budge. Arbe took another step forward. Still, no sister moved. With two more steps, Arbe placed his hand on the shoulder of the lady who answered the door. All seven sisters gasped, as if this was the first time one of them had ever been touched by a man.

Any vow of silence made by the sisters now lifted. "You have violated us, and all the Sisters of Saint Mary-Salome that served before us. How you came to be here at this time, we do not know. What we do know is that you are here, and you are equipped to seize." With this said, the sisters separated.

Now, in clear view, sat a reliquary, the objective of the operation. Preserving the blessed cord for two millenniums, the ornate cedar box rested on top of a table that very well could have been made from the same wood and by the same carpenter. Arbe lifted the box. Another gasp came from the ladies. He handed the reliquary to a team member, who then placed it into a protective container. As the men turned to exit the room, Arbe reassured the sisters, "On behalf of the holy, universal church, *the Cornerstone* will say to you soon, 'Well done, good and faithful servants.'"

As the team headed up the earthy stairs, the video's audio, while faint, picked up a sister's voice. Because she echoed Arbe's parting approbation, Pastor Donovan assumed he misheard her. His family's insistence that he needs hearing aids might have merit, for what he heard was, "And *the millstone* will say to you, 'Well done, my good and faithful servants.'"

* * * * *

The film footage ended, and the lights in the room came back on. George Carlson stood behind the podium and announced, "Men, I present to you the very umbilical cord of Jesus!" And with those words, he removed the cloths, revealing the reliquary just captured on screen. "Inside this small wood box—this one before you adorned with carvings inlaid with gold—rests the cord."

Pastor Donovan sat forward, startled. *Can this really be true? What on earth does George plan to do with it? Is he going to ask me to touch it? How did he know where it was? What happened to the sisters? Why on earth am I here?*

As questions bombarded Pastor Donovan's sense of reality, George leaned forward, and with his hands firmly on the podium, he explained, "I will not bore you with the details, but let me say that cord blood is a rich source of embryonic-like stem cells. In this box, men, is the very DNA of Jesus, perfectly preserved. With the remarkable advancements we've made in our genetic research here at SarkiSystems, the reproductive cloning of humans is not only a possibility, it is in fact a reality." George held up an ultrasound photo of a well-formed fetus. "And here's proof."

George continued, "Just think about it for a minute. We can bring Jesus back. We create an enucleated egg, implant Jesus' cells, stimulate the egg, implant the embryo, watch and pray, and in nine months we witness the second coming of Jesus to this world."

Maxwell, George's co-worker, raised his hand. "I have a question. Isn't human cloning illegal?"

George answered as if rehearsed, "I'm glad you asked this, Maxwell. Yes, our government forbids what I just described. The John Doe fetus I showed you will, I assume, be classified as an 'illegal alien.'" George offered a brief smile, and then got real serious. "The Bible says in the fifth chapter of Acts that the rulers questioned God's men. 'We gave you strict orders not to continue teaching in this name, and yet, you have filled Jerusalem with your teaching and *intend to bring this man's blood upon us*.' Now, do you remember what Peter and the apostles said? They said, 'We must obey God rather than men.' So, Maxwell, yes, I know that what we are doing is illegal. But like God's chosen people have said down through holy history, '*We must obey God rather than men*.'"

George took a deep breath, wiped his forehead, and then resumed to divulge the plan. "Once the baby is born, we can set into motion the fulfill-ment of Ezekiel's prophesy." At this point, the text of Ezekiel 44:1–3 was projected onto the screen.

> Then He brought me back by the way of the outer gate of the sanc-tuary, which faces the east; and it was shut. The Lord said to me, "This gate shall be shut; it shall not be opened, and no one shall enter by it, for the Lord God of Israel has entered by it; therefore it shall be shut. As for the prince, he shall sit in it as prince to eat bread before the Lord; he shall enter by way of the porch of the gate and shall go out by the same way."

After having everyone read together out loud the passage, George carried on, "Today, and for nearly the past five hundred years, this gate remains shut in Jerusalem, completely walled up with guards posted ready to stop the Messiah from entering—all in hopes of postponing the Day of Judgment. But, you and I know that man cannot stop God's plan. Nobody can force the Day of the Lord to wait. The prophecy has been made, the Eastern Gate will be opened, the Messiah will enter, God's kingdom will come, and we shall reign with Him forever and ever. God has promised. It will be so."

George stepped away from the podium and walked directly in front of the men. Pastor Donovan shifted in his seat, looking somewhat bedazzled.

"I know you have questions, a lot of questions. I plan to meet with you to go over all your questions and concerns, and to detail your part in the plan. It's late, and I know you have things to do. I'll see you soon." With this promise, the meeting adjourned.

* * * * *

Pastor Donovan did not say a word as he left the room. When he started up the car, he turned off the radio that's always preset to the Christian station. Inside the car remained quiet, yet anything but peaceful, the entire trip home. The CD of the sermon he preached yesterday caught his attention when it slid across the dashboard as he turned abruptly into his driveway. The soundman had handed the CD to him, just like every Sunday, after the service when he shook his hand. *What could I possibly have said yesterday to help me today?* Not ready to talk about the evening, he headed straight to bed. Though eager to sleep away his cares, he remained wide-awake, attempting to navigate himself out of the maze of his cares. *I'm so lost,* thought Pastor Donovan as he buried himself under the sheets. *I really don't know what to do. If I turn left, then I find that I should have turned right. Whatever I do, whether at church or home or wherever, seems hopeless. If I zigged, then I'm sure I should have zagged. I am lost—stranded, powerless, and doomed to be unworthy.*

In the morning, after eating his wife's "world-famous" waffles with his nose buried in the newspaper, he excused himself from the breakfast table. Sensing something wasn't right, Ashley followed him into the bedroom. "Payne, is everything alright? Is there something we need to talk about?"

"I'm okay. I guess I'm just tired from that meeting I went to last night."

"Then why not lie down for a while?" She fluffed his pillow and reassured him, "I will answer your phone if anyone calls."

He did need time to process what George proposed, so why not do so in bed? To mask this need, and also to relieve a tinge of guilt for doing something so apparently unproductive on a workday, he asked if she would go out to the car and bring him the CD that was on the dashboard.

Using his laptop, Pastor Donovan listened to his sermon. He found himself drifting in and out of listening. Awakened by his dog jumping onto the bed, he wondered, *How many people do I put to sleep every Sunday morning?* Having now drifted back into listening, he heard himself tell the congregation: "Let's do the math. They had five loaves of bread and two fish. This does not add up to feeding five thousand men, plus all the women and children. But let's not forget, they had *one* Jesus. *Now* let's do the math. Five plus two plus one equals *eight*. They all *ate!*" Pastor Donovan smiled as he heard his people's laughter and groans. Then his recorded voice spoke directly to him, "Remember, if you have the one Jesus, then you have all that's necessary."

He sat up in bed and shouted, "*We have all that's necessary!*"

Ashley dashed into the room. "Honey, are you sure you're okay?"

"I'm more than okay. I believe it's finally my time to enter the pool of Bethesda."

"I'm not exactly sure what that means, but it's sure nice to see you re-charged and smiling. Oh, by the way, someone named George called while you slept. He told me to tell you that he would be at the church at two o'clock this afternoon."

Pastor Donovan closed up the laptop, got out of bed, and picked out his clothes for the day. While showering, he sang over and over again the chorus to the hymn "One Day!"—"Living, He loved me; dying, He saved me; buried, He carried my sins far away; rising, He justified freely, forever; one day He's coming, O glorious day!"

2

Pastor Donovan shut the door to his office immediately upon arriving at church. Standing directly in front of his bookshelf, he scanned the books collected from his seminary days. Some he had read, and many he intended to someday. He selected a few from his "eschatology" section. Spreading them out on his desk, he began to research and reacquaint himself with prophesies and timetables. It felt good to turn the pastor's office back into a pastor's study.

George knocked on the door precisely at two o'clock. Having stared relentlessly at the clock on the wall as the time drew near, Pastor Donovan greeted him with praise for his punctuality. "Right on time. Not too many people serve up this common courtesy anymore. Thank you for valuing my time. Please, have a seat."

"I'm sure you have questions from last night."

"It was a lot to take in. How do you know this is what God wants? How do you know this is the right thing to do? It almost seems like an Abraham and Sarah moment."

"Abraham and Sarah?"

"Yes, when Sarah told Abraham to take Hagar as his concubine because Sarah was too old to have the child of the promise."

"Ah—I can see how you might think that—that we are using man-made strategies to try to bring about a supernatural event. But you really don't have the whole story. From SarkiSystems' launch twelve years ago, God has been the One moving things forward. All of the advances in our research and technology have been a result of prayer and listening to God's leading and direction. This is simply the next step in a plan that God set in motion years ago."

"I want to believe you, but it seems too incredible. Besides, what does this specifically have to do with my ministry?"

"Last night I mentioned that we would implant the embryo. For this to occur, we need a womb. Of course, the young girl must be a godly virgin. Our 'Mary' must be one in whom Christ dwells and delights in." George looked right in Pastor Donovan's eyes and announced, "That's why I'm here today. Anne, your daughter, is that girl."

"What?" exclaimed Pastor Donovan. "I don't understand. Are you saying that you want to impregnate Anne? That she would carry your baby?"

"Not mine. God's! Nobody enters her. She remains a virgin. As with Mary, people will count her blessed."

Pastor Donovan stared at him in disbelief. "She's only eighteen. We've got plans. She's got plans. How can she graduate from high school and go to college if she's pregnant?"

"I understand your concerns. But know that the momentary, light affliction that she must endure cannot compare to the eternal weight of glory that awaits her. Yes, her future will change. It will change the world. And hasn't that been your prayer for her ever since she was born, that she would be dedicated unto God and make a difference in this world?"

Pastor Donovan didn't know what to say. How did George know that *that* was exactly their prayer for Anne? Pastor Donovan pondered for a moment the fact that George always seemed to know precisely what he thought and desired. *How does he know so much about me?*

Moving the conversation forward, George suggested, "Last night I promised that you could ask me questions when we met. So, I assume you have a few more questions. I also assume, based on the pile of books there on your desk, that you may even have a few answers."

Though stupefied by George's revelation, Pastor Donovan did smile at the suggestion that he might have answers. He had anything but answers. He wasn't even sure what the questions were to ask. Following an awkward moment of silence, he simply blurted out the first thought that came to mind. "Jesus ascended bodily into heaven. Right? So, because we are told that He will return in the same way, this means that He will return bodily. Visibly, right? However this is to happen, I know that I want to be alive to witness it. Sometimes on our evening walks, especially after I sound off my 'heretic of the week' frustrations for the first few blocks, my wife will look up into the sky and say, 'O, please come, Lord Jesus.'"

"You are not only going to be alive to witness His coming. You are going to help make it happen. You, and especially your daughter, will make a significant contribution to it."

Unsure how to respond or what to ask, Pastor Donovan voiced, "This whole plan of yours is based on a relic. I admit I don't know much about relics, but my impression is that they are 'Catholic.' Once used long ago to generate money, power, and relevance for monasteries and cathedrals, these spectacular treasures from the past now sit tucked away, catalogued and shelved under the Vatican."

George interrupted, "Pastor Donovan, with all due respect, the umbilical cord of Jesus is not some relic, a medieval piece of magic. We're not talking about one of the countless chalices from the Last Supper or splinters from the cross that sustain legends. The Sisters of Saint Mary-Salome vigilantly preserved *the* authentic cord, the one piece of Jesus' body that did not ascend into heaven. We do not have a relic. We have the only true link to the flesh that now sits at the right hand of God the Father Almighty."

Both men sat still for a moment, as if trying to fathom that last sentence. Pastor Donovan broke the silence. "I need time to think about all this."

"Of course," affirmed George. "And you will need to talk with Ashley and Anne." Before Pastor Donovan had a chance to protest or panic, George stood up, leaned across the desk to shake hands, and then said while leaving, "I'll be praying for you."

As George closed the door behind him, Pastor Donovan leaned back in his chair, his hands folded behind his head. *I'll be praying for you.* Pastor Donovan knows that he himself has said this a thousand times to his parishioners. He also knows that many times it has only served as a convenient way to end a conversation. Even as he pondered this flawed spirituality, a flashback from Sunday morning arose. As he walked from the parking lot toward the sanctuary, he saw Brother Bob walking right toward him. Recalling that he had promised to pray for him, he threw up a quick "Lord, help him" just before he greeted Brother Bob with "How are you? I've been praying for you." His pastoral voice of concern surely guaranteed another "homerun."

* * * * *

Regardless of whether George was really going to pray for him, or whether those parting words were an empty promise, an exit plan well played, Pastor Donovan found himself yet again hopeless and lost inside his office, his chamber of desperation. For the past year, haunting episodes of "What's the use?" had invaded his mind. The past week's "When are you going to get more young people coming to church?" comment by his board chairman reverberated through his mind, making him want to lash out with "Well, when are *you* going to do something?" The stacks of conference and seminar notebooks on his bookshelf strangled any leftover hope. Like the slick brochures littering his inbox, they promised the key to leadership and growth, the central but missing program for success. And yet they drove him further into failure and confusion because he couldn't get any "key" to fit. For the past year Pastor Donovan's heart had skipped beats and pounded blood as he sat at his desk and listened to a voice saying over and over again, "Nothing you do will ever matter." Hidden under a pile of thoughts accusing him of being powerless, unworthy, forsaken, and condemned lay a dark wish for God to just take him home. Though carrying this burden, Payne had learned to just keep moving. He managed to pray throughout the rest of the day at church, and especially as he drove home for dinner.

He had already called home to inform Ashley and the kids that they were going to have a "family powwow" that night. So, after dinner, while the kids finished up their homework, Payne invited his wife into their bedroom to have a meeting before the meeting. Behind closed doors, he cautiously broached the subject. "Honey, you more than anyone know that I have been dissatisfied. I've shared about how tired I am of the constant shifting, the endless redefining of success. I'm tired of being inadequate to navigate through the ministry maze."

"Are you giving up?" asked Ashley, the wrinkles between her eyes pronounced with worry.

"No, not at all. In fact, I feel like I'm finally in the game. That low-grade fear of being lost and left on the outside is gone. I feel ready, even ambitious to be *in* on what God is up to." Payne gazed into his wife's eyes, and said, "What I'm about to tell you is confidential. Only those involved are to know. But, there will come a day soon when *everybody* will know."

"Okay, I'm listening," said Ashley as she leaned back onto the bed, using her hands as support.

But, as was often the case when they were in the bedroom, Doug, their son, knocked on their door at the most inopportune time.

"Are we going to have the meeting now?" yelled Doug from the other side of the door. It only took *that* one time of not knocking before entering for him to be well trained to never do *that* again.

"In a minute, son. Do us a favor; find your sister and we will meet you in the living room." Payne looked at his wife and said, "We really do have terrific kids." He paused, then continued with a smile, "You know what they say: fruit doesn't fall far from the tree."

"And neither do the nuts!" grinned Ashley, but not just for her witty comeback. Her countenance conveyed a confidence in her husband.

As Payne watched his wife walk out into the hallway, he wondered for the umpteenth time that day if he was indeed nuts to even consider George's proposal. He knew that, whichever way he turned, fruit would fall. He hoped for good, not forbidden, fruit as he followed Ashley out of the bedroom.

The four met in the living room. Bundt, their chocolate Labrador, laid down next to Anne on the couch with his head resting on her lap—almost as if he sensed what was about to be shared and that she would need comfort.

Payne forewarned, "I want to begin our family powwow by saying that this will not be like any other powwow."

"Does this mean it will be interesting and short?" quipped Doug.

"I guarantee it will be interesting!" How short the meeting will be was not just a good question, it was *the* question. Just how much should be shared? How much should be revealed? Once something was said, it could never be taken back. It would forever change and shape the family trust.

"What I'm about to tell you is confidential. And what I'm about to tell you will, I'm sure, confuse and trouble you. It may even offend you. However, I believe, once you understand and hear me out, it will revive you, or at least intrigue you."

"Dad, just tell us. We can take it." Anne said this in hopes of moving the meeting along. She wanted to return to her original plan for the evening: study for the college admission exam that she was taking on Saturday.

"Actually, Anne, what I'm about to share affects you the most." With this said, and with a deep breath, Payne invited his family to join him as he prayed. They all instinctively bowed their heads. Even Bundt closed his eyes.

"Father, You who loves us with an everlasting love, help us now to wait upon You with reverent and believing hearts. Grant us wisdom and clarity to do Your will completely, cheerfully, and without hesitation. We are so aware that this world is lost, and that You plan to call it to account. We believe that Jesus—the One that was crucified, dead, and buried; the One that rose from the dead, ascended into heaven, and now sits at Your right hand—shall come again to judge the living and the dead. Father, we believe this, and we believe that He could come at any time. Father, more than anything, we ask that You prepare *us* for His return. May we not be distracted, nor cause any delay to our blessed hope. To Your glory and our joy, we pray this in Jesus' name. Amen."

Immediately following the collective "Amen," before the revelation, Doug interjected (Anne rolled her eyes), "Dad, you quoted some of the Apostles' Creed in your prayer. It reminded me of a conversation I had at lunch today at school. One of my friends, who just found out that I am a preacher's kid, asked me if I really believed that Mary was a virgin when she had Jesus. I told him flat out, 'I believe in God the Father Almighty, maker of heaven and earth, and in Jesus Christ His only Son our Lord; who was conceived by the Holy Spirit, born of the Virgin Mary.' My friend laughed at me, called me crazy, and then shouted so all at the table could hear, 'And he believes in Santa Claus and the Easter Bunny.' Everybody laughed."

Ashley chimed in, "Why are people so mean? Why don't people believe anymore?"

"Because they saw their mom and dad put the presents under the tree and the candy in the baskets," chuckled Anne.

"You know what I mean," said Ashley in a tone only a mother could voice. "Why don't people, especially young people, believe in the virgin birth?"

"I don't believe in the virgin birth," announced Anne. Deafening silence filled the room and raised Bundt's ears. She explained, "I believe in the virgin conception, not the virgin birth. The conception was supernatural, but not the birth. The birth involved pain, blood, and pushing. There was no heavenly epidural. It was a natural birth. Isn't that right, Dad? Just like with my birth, there was a birth canal, a placenta, and an umbilical cord. Isn't that what you said in your sermon last Christmas?"

What Pastor Donovan said last Christmas was nothing compared to what he was about to say. *How do you tell your daughter that she was about to become Mary? How do you convince your wife that this unplanned pregnancy is part of God's plan? How will Doug handle his friends' jeering when he defends his sister?* Once again, Payne found himself with no answers, just a growing set of questions that soon would be mute, he hoped.

"You are right. That is what I said." He choked up, paused to catch his breath, and then muttered, "There was an umbilical cord." The family flashed puzzlement, either because they couldn't hear him or because they could. Irreversibly, he candidly addressed his family. "There was an umbilical cord. And that is actually what I want to talk to you about at this powwow. On Monday night, I saw the actual umbilical cord of Jesus."

"Cool," said Doug with excitement. "What did it look like? Did you touch it?"

"No, I didn't touch it. And, well, I didn't actually see it. I saw the reliquary that contains it."

"How do you know the cord was in it?" asked Anne, adding yet another entry into the catalogue of questions.

"It's a bit complicated, but I can assure you that it was. I saw with my own eyes film footage of it being captured from the order of sisters that guarded and preserved it."

"Cool," repeated Doug, now sitting up straight. "Can I watch it sometime? Was there pain, blood, and pushing?"

"No. Now, please, no more interruptions. I want to tell you the unbelievable news. Without going into all the technical details (because, in fact, I don't understand all the science involved), I want to tell you what we plan to do with the cord. Let me just say that, because the blood in the cord is well preserved and well suitable and usable for advanced procedures involving DNA, we can now bring back Jesus. Think about it, for such a time as this, God has graced us with the ability and the means to generate His second coming."

"You can't be serious." Ashley could not help but interrupt. "Are you telling us that you intend to clone our Lord? That you will create Him in some lab? No, better yet, you plan to stage another virgin birth. No, wait, I'm sorry, virgin conception? I bet you already have selected a Mary. Who's your chosen virgin?" Distraught, Ashley pointed toward their daughter, and said sardonically, "Anne?"

"Yes."

"Way cool," roared Doug.

"What?" gasped Anne.

"Are you out of your mind?" Now livid, Ashley stood up and declared that the family powwow was over. She ordered the kids to go to their bedrooms. Bundt followed Anne.

* * * * *

Payne and his wife sat in the living room, staring at anything but each other. When he thought it was safe, he spoke. "Please, Honey, just listen to what I . . ."

"No. You listen to me. My daughter is not going to get pregnant before she is married. She is going to go to college, graduate, get a job that she likes, and then get married to a man that she loves and that loves her and shares her values."

"Just like you. You married a man that loves you and shares your values. I know that I have had more time than you to process this whole thing. But, please, know that what we are talking about will make all things work out together for our good. You know my heart. You also know that I've tried to help the church grow, to move God's mission forward. But I have nothing more to throw to see if it sticks. That is, until now."

"So you're going to throw an umbilical cord?" quipped Ashley. Silence stretched between them—and then Ashley said, "I just don't understand. Is this merely your latest attempt to take the church to the next level?"

"It's not the next level. It's the ultimate level, the pinnacle, the . . ."

"Correct me if I'm wrong, but didn't the devil tempt Jesus from the pinnacle of the temple? And didn't Satan try to use the Scriptures to tempt Him? And didn't Jesus resist him by counter-quoting, 'You shall not put the Lord your God to the test'? Payne, you are not only testing the Lord your God, you are testing your wife with this absurd nonsense. Please, for your sake and mine and especially Anne's, just forget about all this. Go back to being a regular pastor—preach, teach, and run the church—and entrust the results to God." Ashley stood up, staged a consoling smile, and walked to the kitchen, pretending that all was back to normal.

Pastor Donovan walked toward his bedroom to lie down, but stopped when he overheard Anne praying, or at least what he thought was praying. With the door ajar, he glanced in to make sure she was all right. She was not praying. She was curled up on the floor next to her bed, talking to Bundt.

"Everybody has my life all planned out. It seems like ever since I was born I was destined to be smart and to do the right things. Always the student with an A on her report card, and never the girl with an A on her sweater. Don't get me wrong, I'm thankful for what I have. I have you. I remember when Dad brought you home as a surprise. You were so small. When you curled up, just like you are now, you looked just like a chocolate Bundt cake. That's why we named you Bundt. You were a sweet surprise; but you're not the only surprise he has graced us with. Remember when Dad surprised us with a two-week camping trip to the beach. We all thought he was crazy. We were so unprepared and so not wanting to break the family tradition of using Dad's year-long wedding and funeral money to enjoy some mountain resort. That vacation turned out to be the best time together, and we got to take you along, too. Oh, and remember when we . . ."

Pastor Donovan stopped eavesdropping. He plopped on his bed and drifted asleep. Though already exhausting, his day of reckoning continued, for he fell into a dream.

He found himself standing on top of the church's spire. There, up on the steeple, with his feet on the cross, he heard someone yell from down below, "Drop the baby." Much to his surprise, he let go. The baby fell face down toward the ground. But just before it hit the ground it slowed down and then stopped because it was connected to him by a long umbilical cord. The baby bungeed back up toward him. As it returned, it turned over. Now faced up, Pastor Donovan saw that the baby was Anne. She was smiling and saying, "Do it again, Daddy."

He woke up with his daughter by his side saying, "Daddy, I think this is something I should do."

Pastor Donovan shook his head to clear away the sleep. "Are you sure, Precious?"

"If this would really be Jesus' second coming, then what else can I do? It would be wrong to say no."

He hugged her and said, "Don't tell your mother."

3

THE MAIN POINT OF Pastor Donovan's message the following Sunday was that every conversion is a virgin birth, or, as he said more than once to be more accurate, a virgin conception. He shared that being born again was a work of God. "He opens our eyes so we can see. He opens our ears so we can hear. He opens our hearts so we can welcome the gospel." Pastor Donovan explained that this new life, conceived in us like the One in Mary's womb, is by the Holy Spirit. While we are yet doubters and unworthy, God proclaims, "The Holy Spirit will come upon you, and the power of the Most High will overshadow you." Pastor Donovan's eyes and heart fixed upon his daughter as he preached.

He sensed something different about his sermon. His parishioners sensed it, too. *If only these people knew what kind of a week I've just had.* Pastor Donovan could not help but think this as he shook hands at the close of the service. He smiled, but he did not hear his parishioners, except when a few broke from their usual script.

"Pastor, you sure preached with passion today. It really felt like an angelic announcement when you looked right at Anne and said, 'Hail, favored one! The Lord is with you.'"

As he held the hand of this sweet elderly parishioner, Pastor Donovan thought, *If only you knew, Mrs. Gabriel. If only you knew.*

After dutifully listening to a few more customary pleasantries, Pastor Donovan found himself caught off guard when Brother Bob followed up his standard "You really hit a homerun today" with "I'm sure you impressed the search committee that came here today to hear you."

"Search committee? What search committee?"

"That search committee!" retorted Brother Bob as he pointed to the group of four men gathered at the end of the line.

Pastor Donovan's heart skipped. Making their way to shake his hand was George Carlson and the team of men that he met last Monday at Sarki-Systems. "What are they doing here?" Pastor Donovan intended his query to be a mere thought, but Brother Bob heard it.

"That is the question. If they are not a search committee, then who are they and what are they doing here?"

Pastor Donovan did not want to answer these questions. In this case, he preferred questions to remain questions. He spouted rather nonchalantly, "Oh, they're just some friends that showed up to surprise me—and that they have." Eager to curtail further inquiry, he whisked Brother Bob along.

Curious, but not eager, Pastor Donovan anticipated the inevitable encounter about to happen. With his eyes' fluctuating attention on the team, he greeted the remaining few individuals exiting the church. A decoy to mask dismay, he greeted the men with his pastoral voice. "It was a joy to have you here today." He was not about to admit that he did not notice them in church. Though he faced the congregation the entire service, he saw only his daughter in the pew and the distractions in his heart. He smiled and continued, "I wish I would have known that you were coming. I would have asked Ashley, my wife, to have prepared more food for lunch."

Rather perplexed, George asked, "You did not get the phone message that I left last night?"

"No. As a rule, I go to bed early on Saturday nights; and I do not use electronics on Sunday mornings—no phone, no Internet, no television. It is a spiritual discipline to help prepare me for church."

"I called to let you know that we were coming to hear your decision, meet Anne, and to tell you that everything is in place to begin."

With peripheral vision, Pastor Donovan noticed that the family stood ready to go have lunch. What he didn't see was Anne coming to tell him this. She stepped right up to him, leaned her head on his shoulder, and politely interrupted, "Daddy, Mom says the food in the oven will be burnt if we don't leave now." She took her eyes off her dad and turned them toward the men. "Hi. I'm Anne, the pastor's daughter."

"We know."

She looked back at her dad. He cleared his throat, and hesitantly revealed, "Precious, these are the men that know about our surprise. They came to find out our decision."

"Did you tell them?"

"I have not."

Anne stood up straight, faced the men, and declared, "I am willing, and anxious, to pursue the plan."

With muffled elation (for there were lingering parishioners nearby), George said, "That's wonderful! I know that you have questions. That's why we want you to attend our meeting tomorrow night. Your questions will be answered and the Lord's return will be accelerated."

"Will my dad be at the meeting?"

"We would have it no other way." George nodded to the team, indicating that it was time to go. He looked at Anne and said, "Thank you. We'll see you tomorrow night." He looked at Pastor Donovan and said, "And thank you. That was a great sermon."

Pastor Donovan smiled, and then winced when he saw the suspicious look on his wife's face. Even from the parking lot she could make her mistrust known. This was not going to be a normal lunch.

* * * * *

Doug quipped, "It's the way we all like it," when his mom removed the more than well-done roast from the oven. She was not amused by this stock assessment whenever something went wrong in the kitchen.

After the blessing, Ashley immediately asked, "So who were those men that you were talking to after the service?"

"Well, they were not a search committee, if that is what you were wondering." Believing diversion was the best tactic to avoid his wife's inquest, he turned to Anne and asked, "More importantly, how did your college admission exam go yesterday? How do you feel you did?"

Ashley interjected, "I'm so sorry, Anne. I completely forgot to ask you about the test." To her husband's delight, she continued, "How did it go? What was the essay question? I know you were concerned about that part of the exam."

"Actually, I couldn't have felt better about it," responded Anne. "I felt completely free while taking the test, especially while writing the essay."

"That's wonderful."

"But Mom, you know I'm not supposed to talk about the test, especially the essay."

Payne looked down at his plate. Anne had told him about the essay when he picked her up from the test site. "Dad," she had said, "it was like God gave me an opportunity to, I don't know, work things through. I mean, it's not as if the admission exam itself matters anymore. But the question, of all things, asked whether or not our lives would be better off with limitless technology. Dad, I got to think, really think, about what we planned to do. This was my thesis statement: Although many believe that rapid advancement in technology trivializes what it means to be human, I think we should yoke ourselves to it because innovation and expansion are core values for humanity." Still looking at his plate of tough meat, Payne recalled the chill that had gone down his spine when Anne said in the car, "Embrace the future; harness it; and advance it." He wasn't sure if the chill had been from fear or awe.

Doug chimed in as his father sat uneasily silent, "How about a little hint for your favorite brother who will have to take the test in a few years?"

"You want a hint? Here's a hint: Listen to Dad's mantra, 'Catch the wave.'"

Doug was clueless as to what his sister (or his dad) meant by this, except that she was not going to discuss the test any further. He asked if he could be excused from the table. Sister and father caught Doug's wave and exited, too. Mom sat alone in the kitchen. It's the way they all liked it; well, all but one.

* * * * *

Pastor Donovan thanked God for a no-more-questions Lord's Day. He repeated this prayer of thanksgiving the next morning. Ashley would be gone all day with a childhood friend that she recently reconnected with. This meant that Anne and he could go to SarkiSystems without explanation, as long as Doug was distracted. Money to order pizza took care of that.

The room was set up the same. As a pastor, Payne entered with ambition; but as a protective dad escorting his daughter through the door, his first thought was, *Why is there not one more chair set up for Anne?*

George Carlson welcomed the team. With everyone still standing, he announced, "Tonight we place an entry into the book that is in the right hand of Him who sits on the throne in heaven. It's sealed now, but soon this ultimate 'World Civilizations' textbook will be opened."

Dr. Greybellum exclaimed, "In nine months we will see *prosopon pros prosopon* the only One worthy to unroll the scroll of God's sovereign will."

George reigned in the excitement by inviting the men to take their seats. "Indeed, we will see Him *face to face*," echoed George as he motioned to Anne to come to the podium. He prayed a short prayer of grace, mercy, and peace to rest upon her, and wisdom and guidance to be upon the surgeons and all those involved in the procedure. Following a solemn, reverent "Amen," George unveiled the plan for the evening—a blueprint for the team, a bombshell for Pastor Donovan and Anne.

"The embryo implant will take place tonight. In a moment, a surgeon will come to get Anne. An egg will be removed from one of her ovaries. The nucleus will be removed. Using electricity, this enucleated egg will be fused together with Jesus' DNA obtained from the cord blood. The embryo created will be implanted. And then, Lord willing and her temperature doesn't rise, Anne will go home with the Son of Man in her womb."

The body language of both Donovans conveyed uneasiness. They were not prepared for such haste.

George explained that the whole operation would be projected onto the screen. Though no one from the team would be allowed to be present in the laboratory and surgical room, they would see everything taking place in real time. George would narrate the whole affair with the reliquary by his side.

A man in a white coat entered the room from a side door. He motioned to Anne to follow him. Before he knew it, Pastor Donovan was separated from his daughter and the door to her was locked. All he could think about while he watched the screen was that the next time he sees his little girl *prosopon pros prosopon* she will be pregnant, and that someday soon he will have to tell Ashley.

* * * * *

Anne assured her dad, "I feel okay." From the ride home to the days following, she exhibited with each fatherly probe a confidence that mirrored the first Mary. Payne discerned thankfulness deep within her, but mostly relief that the procedure happened so fast. He was not so sure what she might have done if there was a waiting period. He wondered if she would have had a change of heart, like those who abandon their plan to buy a gun, if she would have had more time to think it over. Nonetheless, he knew that it was futile to second-guess the decision and that it was too late to back out. He also knew, as did his daughter, that the next nine months presented a world of hopes and fears, joys and sufferings.

For the moment, while Anne did not show, the surprise could remain a surprise. But could it? How could Payne betray a trust that he had built over the years with his wife? How long could he avoid telling the gospel truth? How long could he hide behind half-truths and diversion tactics?

Anne may not have been showing, but his anxiety sure was, and it was starting to kick.

Pastor Donovan called for another family powwow. He hoped that it would go better than the last one, but it was a tenuous hope. With everyone present in the living room, he stood, ready to speak; yet only silence sounded as he pulled back words. No words were adequate to initiate the meeting. With no pulpit to hide behind and no pastoral voice to bring him honor in this home, he stood inert, petrified in his angst.

Anne stood up, approached her dad, reassured him with a gentle squeeze on the arm, and directed him to sit down. Then with poise, she said to the family, "Exactly one week ago today I became pregnant." She intuitively held her hands out as if to divert verbal harpoons unleashed upon her. "Last Monday Dad and I went to the place where he went the week before—the place where he saw the umbilical cord of Jesus."

Before her daughter could say another word, Ashley insisted, "This must be some April Fool's joke."

"It's no joke." Anne's composure and self-assurance kick started her dad's ability to take the lead. He concisely explained what happened at SarkiSystems. He divulged that one of her eggs was surgically removed, manipulated, and then implanted back into her. The embryo inside her is completely made up of the DNA of Jesus. Like his daughter, Payne held his hands out in defense. He spoke directly to Ashley, "She is still a virgin."

The ensuing exchange entailed words and feelings never before expressed in the Donovan home. Payne tried to intersperse the "what" and especially the "why" during his wife's tirade. When Ashley concluded with insistence that this was no longer, and never was, a funny joke, Anne defended her actions and her dad's. "Mom, I am eighteen years old. I'm an adult. I can and I did make my own choice regarding this. Dad did not force me to do this. It was my decision."

"Will Jesus call me Uncle Doug?"

Ashley turned and stared at her son. "This isn't a joke, Doug." She turned back to Anne. "Do you realize what you have given up? This isn't some dream or nightmare that you can just wake up from."

"Yes, Mom. But I also realize what the world could gain."

"Anne . . ." Ashley stopped and turned to leave the room. As she passed him, Payne heard her mutter, "I wish it were a joke. I wish I could just wake up."

The Cord

* * * * *

Reality hit Pastor Donovan as he prepared for Sunday's message. There in his office he realized that recent events had distracted him to the point that he forgot that Sunday was Palm Sunday. This meant that the choir was scheduled to perform, as usual, an Easter Cantata. Initially, this awakening brought relief. *I don't have to prepare a sermon this week.* Then it brought concern. *Easter, the most attended service, is less than two weeks away; and I am so unprepared. What will I say? What will I not say?*

With anxiety reaching a dangerous level, Pastor Donovan needed a diversion. Whether stemming from a divine illumination or his own human curiosity, he decided to take a moment to figure out Anne's due date. Knowing that her pregnancy began on March 25, exactly one week before April 1 (Ashley's "April Fool's Day" rant chiseled that date onto his mind), and assuming Anne goes full term, he ascertained that the birth would take place on December 25! Was this a coincidence, or yet another one of George's surprises? He double-checked his math. It all added up. The re-birth, the re-incarnation of Jesus was scheduled for Christmas Day. Thoughts flooded his heart. *What a gift . . . to Anne . . . to our family . . . to the church . . . to the world.* He found solace in this diversion, that is, until he got the call.

"This is Officer Bedford. Your wife has been in an accident. An ambulance is on the way to take her to the hospital. She insists, though, on speaking to you. Here she is."

Payne desperately tried to make sense as Ashley cried every word.

"I was listening to the radio and they were talking about abortion and I wondered if maybe Anne's baby could be aborted. But it was such a horrible thought—what if that baby really is Jesus? And then I thought about how it all happened so fast and I wondered if Anne even had a choice in things. I was so angry, so angry at you that I didn't see it. I didn't see the light turn." The words were barely intelligible now.

"Honey, are you hurt?"

The only answer was more crying on the other end of the line and then the officer's voice, "We need to get her to the hospital right away."

"How badly is she hurt?"

"Meet us at the hospital and the doctors will be able to fill you in on that."

Payne opened his mouth, but the officer had already hung up the phone. Slowly, he stood up from his chair and walked out into the little office where the part-time secretary sat, typing up the church bulletin. "Mrs.

Fleury, Ashley was in an accident and I need to go to the hospital." He held up his hand to forestall any questions. "I don't know how bad things are. I won't know until I get to the hospital. Let Bernard know that I won't be able to meet with him about the cantata until later."

He didn't wait to see whether Mrs. Fleury had heard him as he rushed out the door to the parking lot.

* * * * *

Pastor Donovan missed the cantata. The church would have understood if he missed Easter, too, since Ashley had only just been released from the hospital; but he chose to be with his flock and to preach. He was a husband, but he was also a shepherd. Resurrection Sunday brought more people to church than expected, possibly because news had spread about the pastor's wife's accident.

The message focused on Jesus' bodily resurrection in history and how this seals His followers' future bodily resurrection. Knowing that the people knew about the accident, Pastor Donovan spent the second half of the sermon sharing about the frailty of our present bodies. He quoted the Apostle Paul when he wrote in his second letter to the Corinthians that "the outer man is decaying." He shared how the accident reminded him that our earthly bodies are not built to last forever. To curb the tears, he pointed to his balding head and said with a smile, "Hair today, gone tomorrow." He told the congregation that in college he weighed 150 pounds and bench-pressed 275 pounds, but that now those numbers are reversed. He used this humor to convey that our bodies are likened to tottering tents, but he got serious about "the eternal weight of glory" awaiting us. "We will exchange our tents for mansions, bodies fit for all eternity. And what will we do with our incorruptible bodies? We will reign with the One who rose from the dead on that first Easter morning. We will be involved in God's ongoing creative activity—a team effort with eternal significance and productivity." Pastor Donovan looked right at George and the team seated in the back pew as he delivered this last sentence. A glimmer of hope spanned the entire sanctuary. Eternity was in their hearts.

* * * * *

Payne handed his wife the CD of his Easter sermon when the kids and he returned home after church. He was concerned about her state of being and thought that what he said might be medicine for her soul. She laid the disc on the dresser, and then laid her body on the bed.

As Ashley isolated herself from the world, Payne and Anne marched forward on the road of transformation set before them. They could not dawdle until she accepted the reality of Anne's pregnancy. There were decisions to make and strategies to execute.

The team, including Anne, met at SarkiSystems to go over the plan. (Doug stayed home with his mom and enjoyed the delivered pizza.) George explained that Anne would perform her normal routines and graduate from high school. Then, before she began to show, she would go away until it was time to give birth. Forming quote signs with his fingers, he indicated that, when asked, they would say that "Anne is studying abroad" and that "she is expanding her horizon."

George announced to Anne, "You will be going to Israel incognito and on a mission. No one but the team will know what is happening in your womb. While you are in the Holy Land, you will visit various sites. We will film your journey and make a documentary of your pilgrimage."

George then addressed Pastor Donovan. "Let me reassure you that your daughter and the baby will be well protected and cared for the entire time. She will eat well, sleep well, and receive regular prenatal checkups. And you will receive regular updates."

Maxwell queried, "What is the purpose of capturing her trip on film?"

"I'm glad you asked this, Maxwell. Through the use of technology, we will be able to show the world that Jesus has indeed returned. We will, in the fullness of time, broadcast worldwide a documentary of the events that have already taken place—the acquisition of the cord and the implantation of the embryo—along with the events that have yet to take place—the pilgrimage of our 'Virgin Mary' and the birth of our Coming King." Then George avowed that when their efforts were presented, "Every knee shall bow and every tongue confess that Jesus Christ is Lord, to the glory of God the Father."

At the moment, Pastor Donovan was not interested in every knee and every tongue, just his wife's. He knew that Anne's pregnancy and now trip formed Ashley's curse, not confession. He would pastor the congregation, but he would do so without his helpmate, for she walked on her own pilgrimage, a crusade into the castle of despair.

4

PASTOR DONOVAN ACKNOWLEDGED HIS daughter and the other graduates on Graduation Sunday. He congratulated each one by name and said a little prayer for them. For Anne, he thanked God that "Anne is going to study abroad" and that "she will be expanding her horizon."

The next day Anne boarded a plane to Israel. Before she checked her bags, Payne looked her in her eyes, and with tears in his, he said, "I am confident of this very thing, that He who began a good work in you will perfect it until the day of Christ Jesus." With these words from the Apostle Paul's letter to the Philippians, he let go of his little girl—and then returned home to hold tightly his wife.

He entered the summer as he would any uncharted waters, unprecedented events that would test his faith and patience. He prayed for wisdom and strength. His daughter was far away, out of his control—as was his wife. And there was Doug, missing his mom and sister. Wasting no time to set sail into the unknown, Doug asked after the breakfast prayer, "What if she has a girl?"

Perplexed initially, then annoyed, Payne looked at his son, and then he stared at the cold cereal in the bowl. *It's the first day of summer and I already miss Anne, and I miss Ashley's world-famous waffles.* Bracing for the storms lurking on the horizon, he resolved not to focus on the rough waters. He would not be like Peter when he took his eyes off Jesus in the midst of the storm. But this would not be easy. He felt himself begin to sink when Doug bellowed, "Or, what if she has twins?"

* * * * *

What if? Doubt entered Pastor Donovan. What if the plan did not work? What if this was not God's plan? What if something happened to Anne?

When he was just about to spiral down into the place where Ashley resided, the phone rang.

"Hi, Dad."

Payne heard tiredness, but more importantly, joy in Anne's voice as she shared her first report. "The flight went well. I thought that maybe I felt the baby's first kick, but realized it was only air turbulence." The conversation was short because she needed to rest. He could use some rest, too.

He cuddled next to Ashley and whispered, "Anne just called. She sounded good." With this said, he fell asleep with his left arm wrapped around his perfectly still wife, unaware that her eyes remained wide open.

The phone did not ring at the Donovan's home for the rest of the week. Friends were giving them space. Parishioners were off vacationing or making plans to do so. Telemarketers were honoring the do-not-call list. The deafening silence of no long-distance call from Anne caused Payne to more than once check that the phone still worked. *Why hasn't she called? Is she okay? How long will it be between calls? Can I call her?* Questions began to pile up, again. Finally, the phone rang. After a brief pause, a man, obviously reading a script, had an offer that could change his life. So much for honorable salesmen.

Anne called two weeks later. "Dad, so much has happened. I'm sorry that I have not called. We have been so busy, going from one place to the next. But my evening is free. I'm so glad we have a chance to talk."

For the next hour, Pastor Donovan listened as Anne talked about her trip. He smiled as her innocent smile beamed over the phone. She explained that George arranged for her to travel from Nazareth to Bethlehem, making various stops along the way. Her time in and around Nazareth proved to be a memorable start to her pilgrimage. She visited various sites that commemorated Gabriel's annunciation to Mary. Without pausing, Anne transitioned to describing the sense of awe she felt as she walked on the land that Jesus did as a boy growing up. She envisioned Him playing with His friends and working in His father's workshop. The terrain of His neighborhood aroused nostalgia in Anne. The earthiness of Jesus captivated her.

Anne shared about the team's day trip to Cana. She reassured her dad that she did not drink any wine. As a teetotaler and expectant mother, Anne was neither tempted nor vexed by the local merchants' persistent mission to have visitors imbibe history. The excursion caused Anne to reflect on the unique mother-son relationship that Mary and Jesus navigated—and one that they, too, would soon navigate.

She went into detail about how she read and then reflected on the first miracle performed by Jesus. She shared how she had pondered, as she sat outside the church built upon the remains of the house believed to be where Jesus turned the water into wine, *Why is Joseph not mentioned? Was he an absent father like so many are today? Was he dead?* Anne confessed that she could not help but think about her own situation. *Where is the father of my baby? Who is the father? God? George? Is there a father? Am I carrying a mere product of SarkiSystems?* Determined not to wallow in this paternal mystery, she redirected her thoughts to something much more uplifting—Mary's firstborn. "Dad, He was invited to the wedding celebration. It's ludicrous to think that Jesus was always serious. He was fun to be around. Those having a good time welcomed Him." Anne paused, as if receiving confirmation. "Dad, Jesus loved to play. You know how I know this? Children loved to be around Him." Even without a father in the picture, and while tipsy tourists passed by her, she shared how she imagined laughing and playing with her baby Jesus.

Though Pastor Donovan could hear his daughter's grin as she related her Cana experience, he interrupted her, even as she transitioned to sharing how she envisioned herself echoing Mary's instructions, "Whatever He says to you, do it."

"So where are you now?" He injected this question, partly because he wanted to know, partly because he wanted to reassure his daughter that he was still listening, and partly because he just wanted to say something.

"I'm in Megiddo," answered Anne. "But I'm not sure why."

"Many epic battles, biblical and extra-biblical, have been fought there." Pastor Donovan carried the conversation now, explaining the historical and future significance of the place. Sounding more like a preacher than a dad, he explained that this is where the great and final battle of Armageddon would be fought. "Anne, you are at the exact location on the map of the future apocalyptic battle mentioned in the book of Revelation. You are sleeping tonight where the final overthrow of Satan and the antichrist will take place.

As he began to unpack the meaning of the great "Day of the Lord," Pastor Donovan heard commotion over the phone. He heard a man's voice; then he heard his daughter's scream. Then he heard a dial tone.

Frantically, he searched through the kitchen junk drawer for the card he had gotten from SarkiSystems. His fingers shook as he punched in the numbers. The phone seemed to ring forever before he heard a sweet cheerful voice on the other end. "SarkiSystems, how may I help you?"

"I was just talking to Anne—she was on the phone and then she screamed. I need the number for George now."

" George is out of the country right now, but I can see if I can get in touch with him for you."

"You don't understand! She screamed. Something's not right."

"Let me see what I can do, sir. What was your name again?"

"Payne, Payne Donovan. Anne is my daughter."

The line switched to some saccharine love song. Payne clenched and unclenched his hand, willing her to get back to him.

Ten minutes later, the receptionist came back on the line. "Mr. Donovan, I just talked with Mr. Carlson and he said to tell you not to worry. Everything is under control and Anne will call you back as soon as she can. It was just a little misunderstanding."

"But, I need to talk to her. I need to hear her say she's alright."

"I assure you that Anne is fine and will call you as soon as she can. They have quite an itinerary, you know."

Payne realized he would get no further with the receptionist, but he resolved to call back every day until somebody told him something.

Then, for the next two months, he heard nothing—nothing, that is, except echoes of Anne's scream and SarkiSystems' reassurances that all was well.

* * * * *

Pastor Donovan suffered in survival mode, existing as one blinded and trapped by duty and a plan. He preached without care. He shook hands without eye contact. He ate without conversation. He slept without hugging Ashley. Doug summed it up well on the ride to church: "Dad, your sermon title on the marquee at church this week should read, 'Dead Man Talking.'"

The message Pastor Donovan actually preached was on Psalm 121. It was the final sermon in the summer series entitled "Psalmthings to Think About." More so than ever, he needed to hear his own sermon. He needed to be reminded that his help comes from the Lord. The One who made heaven and earth by His sheer word, wisdom, and will is the One who is our keeper. He is our shelter both day and night. Only He could keep us from being smitten by the moon, from going loony. Pastor Donovan found great comfort in the thought that "He who keeps Israel will neither slumber nor sleep." He stated in his message, "God is never exhausted, never weary, never inattentive, never growing old." He ended his sermon by saying, "The Lord keeps Israel, and He keeps the vulnerable that are in Israel. The Lord keeps them from the evil one. He keeps them for His glory. He keeps them in His love. He keeps them 'until the day of Christ Jesus.'"

Then, as usual, Pastor Donovan concluded his sermon with a prayer. What was unusual, however, was the long pause between heads bowing and him praying—praying, that is, out loud; for in the silence he prayed, *Oh, Lord, please keep Anne in Your safe care. Pay attention to her and protect her as she studies abroad and expands her horizon and carries the hope of the world.*

The service ended. The series ended. Sunday ended. Summer ended. Belief was about to end. And then the phone rang on Pastor Donovan's day off, three hours before sunrise. His heart immediately began to race and skip as he leaped out of bed and feared the worse.

"Hello, this is Pastor Donovan." The many phone calls received at this hour had conditioned him to identify himself as "pastor."

"This is George. I want you to know that Anne is back safely under our care. Due to the circumstances of her kidnapping, we could not communicate with you. It would have compromised her rescue and put you and your family in jeopardy."

"Kidnapping? Anne was kidnapped?" Pastor Donovan struggled to understand as he struggled to stand and awaken. As Ashley stirred in bed and returned to sleep, he listened to George give a concise report. George explained that Maxwell, one of the team members, got greedy. "He wanted to serve both God and mammon. He ended up with neither. His 'Judas kiss' cost him his place on the team, and his soul."

"I don't understand."

"Maxwell did not share the same level of commitment as the rest of us. His act of extortion was fueled by greed. He wanted personal power, fame, and fortune. He saw our plan—the return of Jesus for all to see—as a means of great gain. He wanted to control access to Jesus. And, we believe, he wanted Anne. He planned to be her Joseph."

"Maxwell intended to marry Anne?"

"Yesterday, the day we rescued Anne, we found a video file open on Maxwell's phone as he lay dead on the floor in a house on a kibbutz. It documented his intentions. He planned to take Anne as his wife, take Jesus as his son, and together they would take 'The Holy Family' on the road, selling hope from church to church."

No longer standing, but now fully awake, Pastor Donovan asked if he could speak with Anne.

"Not yet, but soon."

"How soon?"

"Tomorrow."

"Promise?"

"Of course. Have I ever let you down?"

For the moment, George's "Of course" persuaded Pastor Donovan that he would indeed get to speak to his daughter tomorrow. However, George's "Have I ever let you down?" would need further persuasion. Not ready to say good-bye, and certainly not ready to go back to sleep, he began to rattle off questions. "How did you find Anne? Where is she now? Is the baby all right? What happened to Maxwell? Why . . ."

George interrupted, "I know you have many questions, but we must end our conversation. I will, though, answer your questions. A chip that was inserted into Anne back at SarkiSystems proved to be a great help in locating her. She is resting outside the city of Shechem. The baby is well. Maxwell took his own life after he refused to surrender." With these terse answers, George said good-bye.

Payne held the phone tightly. With a new set of questions churning inside, he anticipated insomnia—that overstayed, wayward guest in the Donovan home—showing up with even more questions as he sat on the couch awaiting Anne's call.

He awoke the next morning, still clenching the phone, when Bundt jumped into his lap. Like Anne would do, he found himself seeking comfort in the listening ear of their Labrador. "How much do I ask her? Did she see Maxwell commit suicide? How come I did not know about the chip? How much do I tell Ashley? When do I tell the church?" Payne unleashed his heart. Bundt listened.

* * * * *

Pastor Donovan cleared his schedule. He was not about to miss Anne's call.

"Hi, Daddy." These two words, softly and tenderly spoken over the phone, sent tears down his cheeks. It had been too long. Too much had happened. Unable to speak, and desperate to breath, he willed for her to continue.

"I know, Daddy. I love you, too." Anne was barely able to voice these words before her own tears flowed. For the next few minutes, their shared silence and broken sentences spoke volumes. They understood each other. They needed each other. They were more than father and daughter; they were brother and sister in Christ, sharing the blessed hope.

Payne asked Anne about her day. Neither was ready to delve into the horrors of recent events. She told him about her visit to the site of Jacob's well. Though aware that the team resumed the documentary of her journey to Bethlehem, she became lost in her thoughts as she imagined Jesus offering "living water" to the Samaritan woman; then she imagined Jesus offering it to her. She shared, "Dad, as I sat still thinking about this encounter, the baby kicked. For the first time—far more than a brief flutter—I felt His movement. Right there, at the well, Jesus living in me became real. He gave me 'a well of water springing up to eternal life.'"

As she recounted her thoughts, it occurred to Pastor Donovan that her focus was not so much on the woman at the well, as it was on the Man at the well. Jesus' first words to the woman, "Give Me a drink," reminded Anne that Jesus was fully man. "Dad, the Word *became flesh,* and dwelt among us. And He will again dwell among us! We will behold His glory!"

Pastor Donovan treasured Anne's every word. He marveled at her maturity as she continued, "Jesus' last words to the woman, 'I who speak to you am He,' reminds us that He was, and remains, fully God. He is the Messiah, the Lord, *the Word* that became flesh."

As much as Pastor Donovan cherished her day's recollection, he could hear tiredness, even weariness in his daughter. His fatherly advice to "get some rest and eat right" prompted Anne to recount another thought from the day. "Before we hang up, I want to share one more thing that I heard Jesus say there at the well. He said, 'My food is to do the will of Him who sent Me, and to accomplish His work.' Dad, I want this to be true of me, too. Every time the baby kicks, as my own spiritual discipline, I intend to quietly worship *the Father* in spirit and truth. With heart and head, I will be still and know that He is God."

Payne blessed Anne as they said their good-byes. Then he blessed God. Then he went into the bedroom, scooted Bundt off the bed, and hugged Ashley.

* * * * *

Phone calls became frequent and regular when Anne arrived in Jerusalem. There was much to see and share as she journeyed in and around the holy city. From site to site the film crew captured her pilgrimage. From site to site Anne called her dad. After she visited the Wailing Wall, as she rested at a nearby hotel, she called home to share that she had written a prayer on a piece of paper. Before inserting it into a crack in the wall, she read it on camera: "May these people find true shalom. Even so, come, Lord Jesus." She followed this routine outing after outing, week after week. Pastor Donovan never tired of hearing her speak about the places he had only read about in the Bible and preached about in the pulpit. He relayed her stories to Ashley and Doug. This became the routine at mealtime. To his surprise and liking, the Donovans were uniting around Anne's pilgrimage and predicament. Her visits became their visits. When she prayed on the Mount of Olives, they prayed. When she walked down the Via Dolorosa, they counted the cost. Her joys became their joys. Her discomforts became their discomforts. When the baby kicked, they worshiped.

Her questions became their questions. "Why are there two tombs in Jerusalem believed to be the tomb of Jesus? Why is the one that's enshrined in an ornate basilica the one that most tour buses stop at? Why is the one that's outdoors and authentic-looking a mere sideshow viewed with suspicion? In the end, it does not matter. Right? They both are empty!"

"When are you coming home?" As much as Pastor Donovan valued her studying abroad and expanding her horizons, he was concerned that Anne would get too far along in her pregnancy to safely fly home.

"The plan is for me to visit Bethlehem and then to fly home. George reassured me that this is the last stop on our journey until we get back home. Except for what happened up at Megiddo, he is quite pleased with the production of the documentary that will be aired around the world. Dr. Greybellum has provided interesting insights as he narrates the film."

Pastor Donovan had to think for a moment. *Dr. Greybellum? Oh, yes, Professor* Prosopon Pros Prosopon. *How could I forget!* That initial "face to face" meeting at SarkiSystems left a lasting impression, an encounter he could never forget, even if he ever wanted to.

* * * * *

"Bethlehem is not what I envisioned," said Anne over the phone. "I expected to see a humble stable, like the Living Nativity we erect at the church every year. I thought I would experience 'O Little Town of Bethlehem,' but instead merchants mauled me outside the large church that stood over the 'cave' believed to be where Jesus was born."

"Tradition can build barriers and blinders." The instant he said this, questions swarmed in Pastor Donovan's head. *Why do we do the Living Nativity the way that we do it? What other traditions have clouded my own faith and practice? Do any of my beliefs blind me?* There was no time to address the surging questions, for Anne was still speaking.

"Going into the Church of the Nativity brought a welcomed relief from the chaos outside. Walking down the stairs to the cave brought chills to me. Partly because it was cold underground, but mainly because here I was, pregnant with baby Jesus, entering the very place on earth where the Virgin Mary gave birth to Him the first time." Anne described the cave: cramped, cold, and decorated with icons, an altar, and candles. When she finished, she announced, "George has something special planned for tomorrow, and then I'm coming home!"

Pastor Donovan welcomed this good news. Tomorrow they will talk on the phone. The next day they will hug at the airport. Life will return to normal, except Anne will be showing and Jesus will be appearing soon— the new normal!

Discussion at the Donovan's dinner table centered on what they thought George had planned for Anne's last day. Payne supposed that they would hold a big celebration for Anne in Bethlehem. A parting parade and interview would serve as a climax for the pilgrimage and documentary. Ashley offered a more motherly suggestion. She proposed that the team would take Anne on a shopping spree, buying baby clothes *in Bethlehem*. Doug imagined that George arranged to have Anne pose for a portrait that would be used to update Madonna paintings and Nativity figurines. "I hope *she* smiles. Ever notice that Mary is always frowning? Makes you wonder if she secretly wanted a girl."

They were not even remotely close to guessing what George had planned. They proved to be as much in the dark as Anne. She could never have guessed nor been prepared for her last excursion—nor could Pastor Donovan.

Anne's final call came from the airport. She explained right up front that she did not have much time before boarding the plane. In the time that she did have, she shared about her surreal encounter with some nun-like ladies. She described how the team got out of a van behind the Church of the Nativity. They entered a secret passageway, made their way down many stairs, and knocked on an old wooden door. Pastor Donovan's heart raced because of internal questions. *Did she meet the Sisters of Saint Mary-Salome? How did they react to Anne? Why would George do this?*

She continued, "Dad, this old lady answered the door. She looked at my stomach, then directly into my eyes. She did not make eye contact with the other team members. She only focused on my baby and me. We entered a room with candles and icons and an altar-like table. It reminded me of the nativity cave we visited yesterday. The room we were in, if my sense of direction is correct, is located directly below the cave. It's hidden from the public, more than likely because it's been built over multiple times by time and tradition. Except for a few dedicated ladies, the room sits as an abandoned basement, a site unseen."

Pastor Donovan could hear a boarding call announcement in the background. He told Anne that he loved her and would be there at the airport to welcome her home.

"Before I hang up, I want to tell you one more thing about today. When we were in that room, one of the ladies knelt down and wrote on the floor:

> The cord of three
> you shan't overpower
> nor the others resist.
> The cord of He
> shall entangle your heart
> and by force dost exist.

Dad, it was bizarre; for as she did this, I witnessed Jesus—no doubt with my imagination—as He stooped down and wrote on the ground when those wanting to trap Him brought to Him the woman caught in adultery." Anne began to ask about what this might mean, but withdrew the question because she heard the boarding call for those who needed special assistance. "I love you, Dad. I can't wait to see you and Mom and even Doug, and Bundt!"

She said good-bye. Payne imagined her getting on the plane, great with child and with the team. Then he tried to imagine what she imagined when she was with the sisters, but he could not do so. He was too preoccupied with Anne's imminent return to think about anything else, including Jesus' return.

5

"WHERE WILL SHE STAY?" asked Ashley.

"What do you mean?" responded Payne. "She will be here, at home, of course. Why wouldn't she stay here, eat here, and sleep in her own bedroom?"

"What if George has a different plan?"

This one question unleashed a legion of plaguing questions. *What is George's plan? Will Anne be free at home, or will she be sequestered at some safe hideaway? If she is here at home, how will I explain her condition to the church? When do I divulge the plan? Where will the baby be delivered? What happens after He's born? What again is the plan?* Payne raised his hands with palms facing up—a position from which he could either praise God or stop pressing questions from crushing his spirit.

"Let's get her room ready in case she does stay here tonight." This practical advice from Ashley quieted down the questions in Payne's mind, as well as gave them both something to do while Anne flew home.

Doug gave regular updates as he tracked his sister's flight. "The plane has taken off and will climb to an altitude of 35,000 feet." "If Anne looks down right now she will see a big storm below." "My nephew-to-be is still in international waters." "You better hurry up, the plane is scheduled to arrive early." Each update divulged a brother's concern and love.

They all got into the family car, the one purchased after the accident. Ashley turned off the radio as they drove to the airport.

Unlike the pre-nine-eleven days when you could be right at the gate to meet loved ones, Pastor Donovan and the family had to wait outside the baggage claim area to greet Anne. Filled with excitement and anticipation, he did not notice the crowds or the traffic around him. He was focused on one thing: Anne. His plan was to see her eyes, run to her, and embrace her—just like the father with the prodigal son, except that Anne was a daughter and not a prodigal.

His plan changed when he saw George's eyes first. George came right up to Pastor Donovan and the family, and said, "Anne started to have contractions when the plane began its descent. Paramedics are here to take her to SarkiSystems where she will be monitored." As George said this, two men guided a gurney into an ambulance parked right behind them—an ambulance Payne was oblivious to while waiting but now fixated on as it whisked Anne away.

For the moment, there would be no seeing, no running, and no embracing, just Pastor Donovan with more questions, driving the family to SarkiSystems, a place Ashley had learned to loathe.

George greeted them in the parking lot. "Anne is resting now. The contractions have seemed to stop. It would be best for her to get some much-needed sleep. Why don't you come back tomorrow morning? She will want to see you when she's more stable and alert."

Pastor Donovan's tacit approval of George's concern did not diminish his desire to see his little girl. Ashley, however, took this as an opportunity to get off the property. "Payne, let's let her get her rest. Right now, what's important is she's safe. She's home, and you'll see her tomorrow."

* * * * *

The clock in the bedroom slowed down, or seemed to do so, as Payne stared at it. No matter how much he willed the morning to come, time made him wait. Anxiety for tomorrow brought enough trouble of its own for him. He could not sleep. He could not fathom how Doug and Bundt could sleep, snoring away as if the world would go on fine without them. He could not hug Ashley. He could not silence the questions that were well awake in his mind. Then, finally, morning came.

He left to see Anne before his family woke up. He figured they could come later to meet her. Apparently George anticipated Pastor Donovan's early arrival because he stood in the parking lot ready to welcome him. "Anne is eager to see you. Come, follow me."

George led him into the familiar meeting room and then through the side door that Anne passed through to have the procedure. George pointed to a door up ahead and said that she was in that room. Pastor Donovan may not have run, but neither did he hesitate to make his way to the room. Four months may have passed, but now mere seconds would be too long a delay to see his little girl.

He opened the door. There, right in front of him, stood Anne with a big smile, and a bigger stomach. He looked right at her eyes, then at her belly, and then back at her eyes. "Anne, look at you! You are so beautiful." He reached out his arms. "Oh, how I've missed you. I love you."

They embraced with hugs and tears, and then sat on the bed and talked. She talked about the trip, the pregnancy, and the contractions she had on the plane the day before. He talked about the family, the church, and the sleepless night he had last night. Not wanting to miss one thing shared, they listened to each other with both ears and eyes.

The reunion could not have gone better for Pastor Donovan, except for three things. One, he left Ashley and Doug at home. Two, George came in and told him that visiting time was up, even though they were still talking and laughing. And three, once he was able to see beyond Anne, he noticed that the room looked much like her bedroom at home, except that it had plugs and hookups like in a hospital room, and cameras mounted on the ceiling.

Ashley was not amused when Payne got home and described what he heard and saw. "Are you saying she's not coming home? Are you saying I have to go *there* to see my own daughter? If that's the plan, then I want no part of it." With this said, Ashley returned to her bedroom, her portal back to her castle of despair.

Payne realized he would travel alone on the road to SarkiSystems. The next few weeks, leading up to Thanksgiving, established a routine. The new normal for Pastor Donovan included visits with Anne after work, reports about the visit during dinner, and nights without Ashley's companionship; even Doug distanced himself by showing unusual interest in schoolwork. Payne spent evenings listening to news and talking to Bundt.

Visits with Anne also became predictable. They reminisced by playing "Remember When," a game they made up on one of the long family vacation trips. The game is simple: take turns sharing a memory by starting a sentence with "Remember when" and then continuing the game until you want to stop. "Remember when you called a family powwow to tell us about the umbilical cord?" "Remember when you first met George at church?" "Remember when you said goodbye to me at the airport?" "Remember when you walked through that door to have the procedure?" "Remember when . . ."

More so than reminiscing, however, their visits consisted of lamenting current affairs and anticipating the final righting of all wrongs. They talked about the wars and rumors of wars. They talked about the earthquakes and famines around the world. They talked about all the bank closures and product recalls in the news. They talked about how everybody does what is right in their own eyes. At one point, Anne said to her dad, "I know the Bible says, 'Woe to those who are with child in those days.' I could not imagine bringing my child into this world, if not for the fact that my baby is Jesus."

Reminisce about the past. Lament about the present. Marvel about the future. This was the routine, that is, until the water broke. Pastor Donovan and Anne were in her "bedroom" when it happened. This was not the plan. The Christmas Day due date was five weeks away. Before either one called for help, George and a medical team swooped into the room. *Were they watching us? Listening to us? Monitoring every visit?* Payne had no time for these questions. Anne was in labor.

* * * * *

The bedroom transformed into a delivery room. As the doctors and nurses took their places, and as the film crew did the same, Pastor Donovan found himself standing by the door, unable to see Anne. Then he found himself escorted out of the room. George had a chair ready for him in the hallway. For the next few hours he heard a flurry of activity and contraction-delivered screams. He thought he heard George say, "No epidural. No C-section."

Medical talk escalated in the room. Pastor Donovan overheard random words: "monitor," "heart rate," "induce," "cord," "prolapse," "slowing."

His heart beat rapidly and he was having a hard time getting his breath. That was his little girl in there. To calm himself, he got up from the chair that he had occupied ever since the commotion started. To divert his attention, he stood in the hallway, looking at the pictures hung up on the walls. He got lost in hope as he stared at a photo of the reliquary. He marveled at the opportunity it represented, how it protected the faith for such a time as this. *A refuge for troubled times,* he whispered to himself. With Anne's screams in the background, he held tightly to the blessed outcome of their strategic efforts. Still staring at the photo, he thought, *Birth pains are real, but they will be forgotten by morning because of what joy this Child will bring into the world.* He succeeded in distracting himself. He heard his thoughts, and nothing else. No screaming. No commotion. No monitor. No baby crying. The silence became deafening. He turned around to look into the room, but standing directly in front of him was George.

"Anne is stable, but the baby is dead."

Two men, tied together by a common cord, stared at each other.

"I don't understand."

George explained, as if giving a report in a boardroom. "The baby's umbilical cord prolapsed during labor. When we determined that in fact it had dropped into the birth canal ahead of the baby, we immediately moved it in order to relieve the pressure on the cord, the baby's lifeline. What we did not know, until it was too late, was that the cord had wrapped itself three times around the baby's neck."

"The cord became a noose?"

"It suffocated the baby. Because the cord cut off the oxygen, the baby drowned in a sea of amniotic fluid. Apparently, this is why Anne's water bag broke prematurely—to expose that something was terribly wrong."

"This simply can't be. I'm dreaming. I fell asleep in the chair. I will awake to the cry of a newborn—a re-born Savior, who is Christ the Lord!"

"No, you will not awake because you are not dreaming. The baby is dead, but Anne is stable; and she would like to see you."

* * * * *

Still in shock, Payne entered the room. The chair in the hallway now resided next to Anne's bed. He sat down, held her hand, fixed his eyes on hers, and bawled uncontrollably. The only words he could utter while catching his breath were, "You are so special, so precious." Nothing else was said. Nothing else needed to be said.

Through their silence Pastor Donovan could hear the conversation out in the hallway. George was talking with the team, as if formulating an after-action report. He gave instructions to gather all the information and analyze the newfangled cord. "We must learn from this attempt, retool our efforts, and try again."

Not with Anne, thought Pastor Donovan. He now sat next to her on the bed, in position to comfort and protect.

"Daddy, I didn't even get to see my baby," lamented Anne. "This might sound silly, but for months I had looked forward to seeing those tiny little feet. They announced, every time they kicked me in the belly, that peace was coming."

Why would anyone take away the feet of Him who brings good news?
This thought launched a new series of questions to afflict Pastor Donovan.
Why would God have Him, who was brought to life by the cord, die by the
cord? Did the sisters know this would happen? Did they try to warn us? Did
we try to force our plan onto the One who has the prerogative of provision?
What will happen when Jesus does comes back according to God's plan? What
will I say when I stand prosopon pros prosopon *before Him? More impor-*
tantly, what will He say to me?

"Dad, it's late. I want to go home and sleep in my real bedroom."

No one stopped them as they left SarkiSystems. No locked doors
detained them. No cameras followed them. No one seemed to care. They
could return to normal life, if that was even possible.

As they left the parking lot and headed home, Anne asked matter-of-
factly, "So, what are you preaching on this Sunday?"

Her attempt to return to normal life triggered for him the realization
that this Sunday was the first Sunday of Advent. "I'm not sure yet, but it will
have something to do with preparing ourselves to celebrate the first coming of Jesus—His blessed birth—and anticipating His second coming—our
blessed hope."

Anne said nothing, not even a courteous "Sounds like it will be a good
sermon, something for us to think about." Payne turned to look at her. His
heart ached to see the tears streaming down her face.

* * * * *

Relieved to find Ashley and Doug fast asleep, Payne escorted Anne to *her*
bedroom. He tucked her into bed, a bed that for months Ashley com-
pulsively made with fresh sheets and maternal hope. The Donovan's dog
jumped onto the bed as Payne kissed Anne on the forehead and prayed a
brief blessing over her. Bundt settled his head on Anne's stomach, while his
eyes gazed up at his master with a look that asked, "What just happened?
Why is she suffering like this?" Pastor Donovan had no answers, only the
same questions as he left the room.

Fully aware that he could not sleep, and that he would not sleep so as
to be ready to attend to his daughter if necessary, Pastor Donovan sat alone
in the kitchen. He kept the kitchen door slightly ajar so he could hear any
cry for help and closed enough so the light would not shine down the hallway. A note on the table informed him that dinner was in the refrigerator.
Though the turn of events at SarkiSystems prevented him from partaking

in the evening's dinner and discussion, he found himself not hungry—at least not for the food ready to be heated up in the microwave.

What he hungered for were answers, insights that would feed his famished spirit. By coincidence, on the table, next to the note, lay Ashley's Bible. Pastor Donovan opened it to where his wife had bookmarked: the book of Lamentations. Highlighted on the page were three verses from the third chapter:

> This I recall to my mind, therefore I have hope. The Lord's lovingkindnesses indeed never cease, for His compassions never fail.
> They are new every morning; great is Your faithfulness.

Pastor Donovan stared at these words. Two words—"every morning"—stared back at him. With them highlighted on his heart and the clock on the wall ticking in the night silence, his thoughts fixated on the encounter about to happen when Ashley awoke. *Every morning? I'm not asking for every morning, just this morning. My confusion and guilt is about to consume me. Lord, I need Your mercies now!*

A sudden but brief sound of stirring in one of the bedrooms diverted Pastor Donovan's train of thought, as well as unsettled his body. Up out of his chair, but not needed in another room, he noticed Ashley's bookmarker in his hand. On it were the words of the Lord's Prayer, words that often nourished his soul. Standing at the kitchen table, he prayed the prayer, feasting on every phrase. As he recited "Give us this day our daily bread," he thought about and then gave thanks for the dinner in the refrigerator. After the "Amen," he heated up his wife's world-famous chicken and rice casserole. For now, his body and soul found food, but more hunger pains were about to dawn.

* * * * *

Pastor Donovan heard crying as he awoke. Gathering his thoughts and his nerves, he pushed the chair away from the kitchen table, away from the empty plate and open Bible. He prayed every step to Anne's bedroom. He initially stopped at her door, faced his ladies and his fears, and then entered the room. Ashley and Anne were clutching each other, expressing "I love you" without words, only tears. Payne understood that this was not the time to talk about what happened, and certainly not the time to suggest a way to fix it. He simply retreated with empathy back to the kitchen, expressing heart-wrenching emotions and ideas in a language too deep for mere words.

"Dad, what are you doing?" asked Doug as he pored milk into a bowl of cereal. "Were you just speaking in tongues?"

"What? No."

"Then you must have been speaking in grunts!"

Speaking in grunts. Pastor Donovan reflected on Doug's offhand, yet spot-on description. He also considered that, once his son finished breakfast, he would need the gift of interpretation.

"Doug, Anne is home. She went into labor yesterday, but there were complications. We will need to give her time and space to rest and recover."

"Where is the baby?" asked Doug. "Was that Jesus I heard crying earlier?"

"No, that was your mom and sister." Payne placed his hand on Doug's shoulder and unveiled, "The baby did not survive the birth."

For a moment Payne thought Doug was about to speak in grunts, but instead his son reiterated, "Where is the baby?"

His son's question and tone confused him. "Are you asking me where babies go when they die?"

"No! I know baby Jesus is in heaven. What I want to know is, where is His little body? What happened to it?"

Payne had no answer, no idea as to what happened to the baby. *Did George dispose of the body? Did he give it a proper burial or did he retain it for research's sake?* "Son, I'm sorry, I can't answer your simple question because I don't know." He paused, and then said, "But I promise you this, I *will* find out."

6

PASTOR DONOVAN DREADED THE immediate days following Anne's return home. He constantly feared saying something wrong, something insensitive, something that would catapult one or more family member into a dungeon of despair. He feared the pulpit, too. He knew his parishioners would come with great expectations on Sunday, the first Sunday of Advent. He knew he would come with great apprehensions. If honest, he would announce, "The first candle I light here today is the candle of desolation, not hope." How could he talk about confident expectation when his confidence and expectation had disappeared, lost somewhere in his hopeless maze?

Pastor Donovan drove by himself to church on Sunday morning. His family stayed home, not yet ready to face people, not even with the masks they stored with their Sunday best. He, however, ready or not, masqueraded through the service. He pulled from his sermon file the first message from an Advent series he preached five years ago. He remembered that he liked it, but he did not remember the content. His hope this Sunday was that his people would not remember either, but would like it.

Pastor Donovan shook hands at the door following the service. With mixed emotions he listened to his people offer their usual praise. He was pleased that no one confronted him on his repeat performance, yet disconcerted that no one remembered. After the last person filed out to the parking lot, Pastor Donovan headed straight to his office, straight to his filed-away sermons. Because distractions awaited him at home, he wanted to make sure that his notes for the rest of the series were in order. Satisfied, though feeling a bit guilty, that his sermon preparation was nearly complete for the next few weeks, Pastor Donovan headed out the office for home.

By the time he reached his car in the church parking lot, however, the touch of guilt that he felt in his office now held a firm grip on him, choking his ability to think about or do anything else, including driving. Sitting in front of the steering wheel, he mulled with self-reproach, *I must at least read the text of the series. If I'm not going to take time to study and meditate on it, I should at least take time to read it.* To loosen the paralyzing shame—and to obey the voice that whispered "Then why not now?"—Pastor Donovan picked up his well-worn Bible that he had placed on the passenger seat and read out loud First Timothy 3:14–16.

> I am writing these things to you, hoping to come to you before long; but in case I am delayed, I write so that you may know how one ought to conduct himself in the household of God, which is the church of the living God, the pillar and support of the truth. And by common confession great is the mystery of godliness:
>
> He who was revealed in the flesh,
>
> Was vindicated in the Spirit,
>
> Beheld by angels,
>
> Proclaimed among the nations,
>
> Believed on in the world,
>
> Taken up in glory.

Advental hope, peace, joy, and love came over Pastor Donovan as he read and re-read this early Christian hymn. As if a divine breeze entered through the windows and vents of these timeless truths, each line refreshed his troubled spirit. From "He who was revealed in the flesh" to "taken up in glory," the common confession reminded him of Jesus' humanity and divinity. Oscillating between the mind-boggling descent and ascent of Jesus, His earth-ness and heaven-ness, Pastor Donovan's mind and heart cried out, *How can I not trust You to work everything out? The Holy Spirit upheld and defended You throughout Your life, death, resurrection, and ascension. Will He not also do so when You—the infinite that became an infant—return?* As he pondered the fullness of Jesus, a thought burst into his mind, *Maybe SarkiSystems plays no part in the pillar and support of the truth. They've had no contact, no words of comfort or explanation for us in the last few days. At least Sarah talked to Hagar after her plan failed. But everything works together for good, right?* Unbeknownst to the few parishioners lingering in the parking lot, Pastor Donovan's vision of God's rule and reign expanded. The car had morphed into a sanctuary, a thin place where God graced him with a momentary glimpse of His glory. Engulfed in God's greatness and grace, he started the car and drove away in his mobile refuge of strength.

* * * * *

Pastor Donovan savored every bite of the Sunday meal awaiting him when he returned home—not so much because the chicken enchilada casserole was not burnt, but because Ashley and Anne prepared it together. The family was back together, eating, talking, and even laughing.

"Did you give them heaven today, Dad?" asked Doug.

"I did, and a little earth, too." Payne smiled as he observed his son's bewildered face, and as he asked his wife for a second helping of her world-famous dish. "Today we focused on Jesus being both God and man, and how the church is a pillar and support of this truth." Before he could rehearse the main points of his Advent series, Ashley and Anne announced that there would be a family powwow once the table was cleared and the dishes were washed. *Obviously more than just cooking happened in the kitchen while I was at church,* deduced Pastor Donovan. *My ladies have been talking, but about what?* He was about to find out.

"We would like to have a memorial service tomorrow." Ashley wasted no time in coming to the point of the family meeting. "Anne's baby deserves our respect and we need to mourn our loss." Reality hit Payne hard as his wife shared how they needed to mourn, how they needed to create some space and time to address their loss. Confronted by deep emotions surfacing for the first time, he feared a complete breakdown right there in the living room, right there in front of his family, right there in front of the very ones who needed him strong. But the sorrow proved to be too painful, too real to be hidden. Payne noticed that even Doug's eyes leaked tears; though if he inquired, he was sure that his son would say that it's just his allergies acting up.

Anne shared what she would like for the service. She suggested, as part of the healing process for the family, that they plant an olive tree in the backyard in remembrance of her baby. "The service, if it's alright with you, Dad, and you, Doug, will be held in the backyard tomorrow after dinner. Each of us can share what's on our minds and in our hearts. And Dad, I would like for you to bring a brief message like you would at a normal funeral."

At a normal funeral? I may have done a few funerals for stillborn babies over the years, but this is different. Pastor Donovan's thoughts swung back and forth on a pendulum of emotions. *How can I possibly say something tomorrow to help bring healing and comfort? How can I possibly not?* He may have next Sunday's sermon well in hand, but he knew there was no sermon filed away for what awaited him tomorrow.

Not much conversation took place following the powwow. Pastor Donovan remained seated on the couch as he watched each family member drift into their corner of the house, their personal rehab center. Then, with his Bible in hand, he headed out to the car parked in the driveway. He wanted to be alone, away from the home phone and any other distractions. He wanted to be where he could have his breakdown, where he could cry like a baby for the baby. He wanted to return to his place of refuge.

What he encountered, however, was a knock on the car door. Ashley and Anne wanted to go to the nursery to buy an olive tree. Doug wanted to know where the shovel was and where he should dig the hole for the tree. Payne complied with their needs and headed back into the house where he encountered Bundt scratching on the back door. As he complied with his dog's need to be let out, he could hear the faint sound of the car backing out of the driveway and the shoveling of dirt in the backyard. There, alone in the service porch, without warning or control, Pastor Donovan leaned against the washing machine and bawled like a baby—or rather like a man lost and desperate to have his Father hear him and find him in the cosmic maze.

* * * * *

Monday started off solemn at the Donovan's home. Breakfast consisted of leftover enchiladas and eggs that Ashley prepared early in the morning and left in the frying pan on the stovetop. Having changed his day off, Pastor Donovan went into work to shuffle a few papers on his desk, return a few phone messages left on his voice mail, and write a few notes for next Sunday's bulletin. His attention, however, while doing these pastoral chores, remained on the pending memorial service. Drifting between razor-sharp focus and paralyzing worry, relentless questions flooded his mind. *What on earth do I say? Do I have anything meaningful to offer? Or do I just have platitudes, pithy but superficial clichés rendered with a pastoral voice? What scripture passage should I read? Is there anything I should not say, any issue I should avoid? What again is the purpose of this service? Is it really necessary?* These and countless more questions kept Pastor Donovan busy and serious throughout his day at church and on his ride home.

Dinner involved polite conversation, perfunctory "bless the food" and "pass the salt" manners. Though he skipped lunch, Pastor Donovan only served himself a small portion, and even then he could not finish what was on his plate. He noticed his family's loss of appetite, too. "Honey, thank you for fixing dinner. Why don't we all just leave the dishes on the table and get ready for the memorial service? Let's meet in the backyard in five minutes. Okay?" All heads nodded, indicating consensus and relief.

Pastor Donovan instinctively picked up his Bible from the coffee table in the living room and made his way out the back door, allowing a flashback of his breakdown to momentarily interrupt his intention to be present and ready to welcome his family.

"Tonight we remember a life. Tonight we look for hope and peace from the One who gave us that life." With these words from Payne, the service began.

Before he could offer up an opening word of prayer, Ashley interjected, "So to help us remember Anne's baby, we will plant this tree into this hole and together watch it grow over the years to come." She and Anne placed the tree into the hole, and Doug packed dirt around it. Payne simply watched *and* discovered that he was not in charge of this service. Ashley turned to him and said, "Now would be a good time for you to pray."

He launched intuitively into a prayer that he began most funerals with: "Heavenly Father, You who loves us with an everlasting love, help us now to wait upon You with reverent and believing hearts. In the silence of this time together, speak to us of eternal things, that through patience and comfort of the Scriptures we may have hope, and be lifted above our darkness and distress into the light and peace of Thy presence. Amen."

Immediately following the echoed "Amen," Ashley stated, "Thank you, Payne. Now we will each share what's on our minds and in our hearts. We will start with the youngest and finish with the oldest."

"Does this mean Bundt goes first?" Since nobody seemed to appreciate his wit, Doug cleared his throat, looked at Anne, and began, "I never told my friends about you being pregnant. Not because I disapproved or was ashamed, but because I did not understand what happened to you. If I don't yet get the birds and the bees, how in the world can I explain the cords and the clones? What I do get, however, is that it must hurt a lot. I see it in your bloodshot eyes. Even though I will never carry a baby in my belly (though SarkiSystems may concoct a way for *that* to be possible), I tried last night to imagine how you must feel. It sucks, doesn't it? You feel the baby, care for the baby, and then the baby's gone. And what do you get to take home to cuddle? Painful memories and shattered dreams. Sis, that sucks."

Witnessing a rare brother-sister hug, Pastor Donovan curbed his disapproval of his son's use of the "s" word. *Now is not the time to discipline,* he thought. With Anne about to speak, he resolved, *Now is definitely not the time.*

"It does suck. I not only lost my baby; I lost my hope." Overcome by her pain and shame, Anne dropped her head into her cupped hands and wept. Distraught but determined, she continued. "I am so angry. I am angry with you, Dad. You should have protected me from, not presented me to, George and his 'plan.' And Mom, where were you when I needed you? How come you gave up so easily and didn't fight for me? You left me. You left us. But, of course, I'm more angry and upset with George and the entire team at SarkiSystems. How dare they use me like they did? How dare they discard my baby and me? May God discard them all if they ever try their experiment on another girl! And speaking of God, I'm most angry with Him for taking my baby. What kind of God rewards faith, hope, trust, and confidence with this, a tree in the backyard? A loving God would have given us a life to love."

And a swing to play on, not a plant to water, in the backyard, thought Payne as Anne regrouped. He noticed that her countenance improved having expressed her built-up anger. *Maybe this is a part of the healing process for her*, he reasoned, *and for the rest of us.*

"Are you done, Anne?" asked Ashley.

"No."

"Oh, great," snapped Doug. "Now she's going to aim her anger at me."

"No," asserted his sister. "If anything, I want to thank you for being you. You are unpretentious, even when you're not so sure—and with that look on your face, evidently even when you have no clue!"

After a family chuckle, Ashley said, "Anne, what else do you want to say?"

"I am angry. I've made that clear. But I don't plan to stay angry. Oh, I'll keep righteous anger, but I'm pretty sure that what I have now is mostly unrighteous anger. I don't have the character to handle the resentment. You'll mostly find revenge-filled rage roaming in my heart these days. More importantly, I need you to know that I have lost hope. I plan to find it again. And when I do, I am sure it will not be the same. My hope will be wiser and stronger, a hope that I will be willing and able to live with and die with and give to others. I don't know how it will come, but I am willing to find out and pretty sure it will come knocking serendipitously at my door." Anne motioned to her mom that she was done. But then, as an aside, she looked at Doug and said with a grin, "If you don't know what 'serendipitously' means, then I'm sorry that the magnitude of my expression was too copious for your immediate comprehension."

Pastor Donovan smiled as Anne used on Doug the very remark that her brother uses when he knows someone didn't understand what he said. Payne's smile continued as he witnessed his wife, the one in charge, extend grace to their daughter for her last comment. With Ashley's turn to speak next, he wondered if she would extend the same grace to him. Hidden fear inhabited his heart. *What will she say? Will she reveal what's really on her mind and in her heart? How much will be directed at me?* As Ashley gathered her thoughts, Payne's questions spiraled down into beseeching lament. *Oh, God, how badly have I screwed up?*

Staring at the olive tree, Ashley commenced, "This is not what I wanted to happen. This is all wrong. We should never have done this."

"Honey, you're the one who suggested it," interjected Payne, thinking his reminder would tactfully instruct her back to the task at hand, back to why she asked to have the memorial service in the first place.

"What?" His ill-advised reminder sent Ashley into a tirade. Now glaring at her husband, Ashley let loose thoughts previously unspoken. "This whole thing is your fault. How could you have ever thought that this was God's will? Where in the Bible does it ever tell you to do what you did? Did you have some angelic visit or announcement, a direct word from God? How could you rope our daughter into this plan? You betrayed my trust. You never asked me what I thought. You never do. You always run ahead of me, force-feeding your idiotic endeavors on me and the family. Why? Do you like playing the fool?"

With this said, all four Donovans were back staring at the tree. No one dared to say a word, especially Payne. He did, however, grapple with the thought that his turn to speak was next. *Is she finished? Does she really want me to answer her questions? They're rhetorical, right, answered already in her mind?* For the time being, he simply looked straight ahead at the fruitless tree, banking on the proverb that even a fool looks wise when he keeps his mouth shut.

"How could you go behind my back like you did? Is that what you counsel the men at church to do? 'Keep your woman in her place; make sure she knows you're her head, her master, her savior'? And how could you involve your own daughter? Were you training Anne for the life awaiting her? 'Precious, this is how men will treat you, this is your God-ordained role'? Were you catechizing her with 'The chief end of woman is to glorify her man and endure him forever'?"

From his peripheral vision, Payne could see Ashley wiping tears from her eyes, cheeks, and neck. She was speaking in tears, tears begotten in the whitewashed sepulcher of a betrayed marriage. On the outside, from the perspective of the church members, their marriage looked ideal, two people there for each other in times of need. From the inside, however, from the perspective of the four standing in front of the olive tree, this marriage and family was decaying right before their eyes, wasting away like a loved one on life support.

"What did you name him?" Doug broke the difficult silence with this innocent question. "We're here at his memorial service, and yet we have yet to say his name."

Until his son's inquiry, Pastor Donovan had resigned to avoid eye contact with Ashley, his inflamed wife. But now, facing her with stunned guilt, he looked to her for the answer. But seeing the dumbfounded look on her face, he turned to Anne and said, "I am so sorry, Anne. I never asked you. I've been so concerned about how I would get us through all of this and what I was going to say tonight that I never even found out what you named your baby. Your mom is right, I am a fool."

"Joshua."

With Anne's announcement, Pastor Donovan turned back to his wife and said, "Joshua! Did you hear that? She named him Joshua." Tears formed as he reflected, "Honey, our first grandchild, she named him Joshua."

Doug asked, "Why didn't you name him 'Jesus'? I like 'Joshua,' but, I'm curious, why not 'Jesus'? Why 'Joshua'?"

"Both names mean 'God saves.' All along I believed God was going to raise up my baby to save us from this world. The past few days, after his death, I prayed that God would save my baby; raise him up like He did His only begotten Son. But it's been more than three days, and for all I know, he's still dead; and so we have this olive tree instead."

Payne still heard anger and battered hope in Anne's voice as she shared, but he also heard a mother's love. "Just last night I was sitting on my bed talking to Bundt about Joshua. I told him that there was a book in the Bible named after him—Joshua, that is, not Bundt." She looked at her brother and smiled as she clarified herself. "I began reading chapter one of the book of Joshua to Bundt. I explained to him how God charged him—Joshua, that is—with a mission. And how his leadership would bridge old tradition with new tradition; how there would be continuity with the past *and* the new tasks and experiences of God. Bundt was a good listener as I talked about Joshua and read the opening verses. When I got to verse nine, however, I felt like I was now the one being taught and read to—by God. It was as if He directly said to me:

> Have I not commanded you, Anne? Be strong and courageous!
> Do not tremble or be dismayed, for the Lord your God is with you
> wherever you go.

Whatever awaits me in the future, I believe God wants me to hold tightly to these words, to carry them in my heart for the rest of my life. I sat there on the bed with Bundt and thought, how ironic, that God delivered my life's verse through my baby's death."

"Did you give Joshua a middle name?"

"No, Doug."

"Then how about 'One-Nine'? Joshua One-Nine Donovan."

Anne smiled at her brother's suggestion, then reiterated, "For now, I am dismayed. I do tremble. I am angry. I need hope." With this said, she addressed her father: "That's why I so want to hear what you have to say. I so need to hear God speak through you."

Though he had considered and agonized over this moment, Payne stood before Anne as one lost—lost in a sea of guilt and shame, lost in a maze of regrets and fears. And, he stood as one lost for words, paralyzed before the promising yet barren olive tree. *What kind of pastor has nothing to say in a time like this?* Outwardly he remained still and silent, but inwardly he wandered and spoke to himself. *What kind of father would do what you did to your daughter? What kind of husband would do what you did to your wife?* His self-talk ultimately transitioned into prayer. *Lord, forgive me. Save me from my foolishness.* Lost for words even in his thoughts, he borrowed King David's "sinner's prayer," words from Psalm fifty-one he memorized long ago. *Be gracious to me, O God, according to Thy lovingkindness. Wash me. Cleanse me. For I know my transgressions, and my sin is ever before me. Create in me a clean heart, O God, and renew a steadfast spirit within me. Do not cast me away from Thy presence, and do not take Thy Holy Spirit from me. Restore to me the joy of Thy salvation, and sustain me with a willing spirit. Then I will teach transgressors Thy ways, and sinners will be converted to Thee.*

For a brief moment, triggered by David's latter words, Pastor Donovan thought about George Carlson. But before burying himself in that rabbit trail, he regained focus with Ashley's directive, "It's your turn, Payne. We're waiting."

Pastor Donovan cleared his throat and opened his Bible. Unsure of what exactly he would say, and, if truth were told, of what exactly he would read, he settled on the opening verses of the twenty-first chapter of the book of Revelation. "The verses I'm about to read describe the new heaven and the new earth awaiting Joshua and all of God's chosen people. Let us, then, hear the word of the Lord as it is brought to us in the second to last chapter of His holy scripture, our final authority for faith and practice:

> I saw a new heaven and a new earth; for the first heaven and the first earth passed away, and there is no longer any sea. And I saw the holy city, new Jerusalem, coming down out of heaven from God, made ready as a bride adorned for her husband. And I heard a loud voice from the throne, saying, "Behold, the tabernacle of God is among men, and He shall dwell among them, and they shall be His people, and God Himself shall be among them, and He shall wipe away every tear from their eyes; and there shall no longer be any death; there shall no longer be any mourning, or crying, or pain; the first things have passed away." And He who sits on the throne said, "Behold, I am making all things new." And He said, "Write, for these words are faithful and true." And He said to me, "It is done. I am the Alpha and the Omega, the beginning and the end. I will give to the one who thirsts from the spring of the water of life without cost."

Pastor Donovan stopped reading after verse seven. He did this for two reasons. First, he felt like God gave him something to say, a word for the family. And second, he did not want to hear what God had to say in an upcoming verse about the "cowardly," "abominable," and "liars."

"Anne, Ashley, Doug—when I began reading this passage, I envisioned that after I finished I would highlight that there is coming a day when God will wipe away our tears; that there is coming a day when there will be no death, no crying, no pain; and that, most importantly, God will dwell among us and we will be His people in that day. All this is true and can bring hope to us at a time like this. But it's the first description of this new heaven and new earth that I believe God wants us to focus on here at Joshua's memorial service. He tells us that 'there is no longer any sea.'"

"But I like the sea," chimed in Doug. "Why would God not let us have a sea to play in and to look at? I could understand 'there is no longer any school' or 'no longer any Brussels sprouts.' But 'sea'? I don't get it."

"We have to understand that the sea for people back then was a place of mystery. Back then they did not know what lurked down below. They had no submarines, no Jacques Cousteau to help them fathom the oceans. The sea stirred fear and terror in the hearts of man. The sea was believed to be the hideout for evil, the dwelling place of opposition and chaos. The sea also symbolized a life of unrest—one moment it is smooth like glass and the next moment there's turbulence; one moment your life is at peace and the next moment you're in the midst of a violent storm or facing an imminent one on the horizon. And one more thing for us to remember: for John, the one who wrote Revelation while exiled on the island of Patmos, the sea was what separated him from his loved ones."

"So 'the sea' symbolizes what sucks here: our unanswered 'whys,' SarkiSystem's unfathomable evil, Joshua's untimely death, and God's un-welcomed distance. Is that right, Dad?"

"That's exactly right, Doug. For now, on this side of eternity, we have questions, evil, unrest, and excruciating goodbyes to face. But there is coming a day when God will put an end to this 'sea' of suffering."

"He'd better," said Anne, "otherwise, there is no hope for anyone. Thank you, Dad, for giving me something to think about. Whenever I think about Joshua or look at this tree, I'll try to take to heart what you said about 'there is no longer any sea.'"

"I can live with 'no longer any sea,'" said Doug. "And I could live with 'no longer any school,' too."

Ashley said nothing.

Sensing that his wife had relinquished her role to officiate, Payne took it upon himself to close the memorial service with prayer. "Eternal God, You are the Source of life and the Comforter in death. Thank You for Joshua Donovan. Grant our family wisdom and strength. In our confusion and grief, provide us comfort. In any feelings of guilt or regret, reassure us of our worth. We come here to mourn the loss of Joshua, to hold out and endure his absence, not to replace it. We turn to and look to You for help and hope as we voyage through this sea-plagued life until that day when we too will be committed to earth's grave—earth to earth, ashes to ashes, dust to dust. Amen."

Pastor Donovan remained outside as the family quietly and dutifully returned to the kitchen. As he heard dishes being cleared from the table and rinsed in the sink, he gazed intently at the tree in front of him. That is, until an airplane on its approach to the nearby airport distracted him. Watching the plane fly overhead, he wondered what awaited the passengers when they landed. *What storms will they encounter? How many are coming home, reuniting with family and friends? How many are about to be as far away as they ever have been from home, separated from loved ones? Which ones will play the fool? How will the ever-looming 'sea' affect their lives?* Pastor Donovan's own plane landed—he returned to his own story—when he heard his wife yell out the window, "We could use your help in here."

7

THE NEXT FEW DAYS at the Donovan home resembled a case study in de-
nial. As a coping mechanism to process and adjust to their distress, each
family member took on obsessive-compulsive assignments. Ashley deep
cleaned the kitchen and organized the hall closets. Doug watered the olive
tree and everything else in the backyard. Anne rearranged her bedroom
and groomed Bundt. Pastor Donovan buried himself in random news stories and incidental errands. Each fulfilled their self-assigned tasks dutifully
and repeatedly.

Bundt looked and smelled good when the family finally sat down together to face the future, to address the inevitable "Where do we go from
here?" question.

Pastor Donovan led the powwow. "Before we consider what's next, I
want to, no, I *need* to be honest with the three of you. Anne, you confessed
that you are angry. Well, I confess that I am lost. I feel useless and out of
place—as a father, husband, and pastor. I know I'm not where I'm supposed
to be. My family, my marriage, and my calling are like a lost set of keys. I
must find them."

"We're right here, Dad," grinned Doug.

"Let me explain. The other night, after the service, I was taken by an
airplane flying directly overhead." Pastor Donovan paused, looked at Doug
and clarified, "Not literally—it didn't beam me up—but it did make me
think. Even though planes daily fly over our house because it's on the flight
path to the airport, for some reason, and I don't know why, *that* plane captured my thoughts. I just can't get that plane out of my mind. I wonder, who
was on it? What lies in store for them? Will one of them be in the news?
Will they have fifteen minutes of fame or move about without anyone noticing? Will their stories interact with our stories?"

Ashley muttered, "Who knows?"

"Exactly. Who really knows? That's really the question, isn't it?" Eager to use this as a transition to his next thought, Pastor Donovan looked and sounded a bit lost. "Nobody knows our real stories anymore. We keep a safe distance away while we project our image. Like looking up at the plane, my parishioners look up to me and see a pastor and church moving along just fine; but what they don't see—and I don't want them to see—is the great turmoil in the cockpit. They see that attendance is up (or at least steady), giving is up (but could be better), and buildings are up (with a few in need of repairs). But what they don't see is the commotion around the controls. What they don't see is that their pilot is no longer flying the plane. What they don't see is that we're about to crash."

Payne paused to catch his breath and his nerve, then he addressed Ashley, "You are right. I have played the fool and allowed a radical plan to overtake me and our family. Please forgive me." He scooted over to her on the couch, took her hand, looked up and prayed out loud: "Forgive me. Restore us. Give us wisdom and strength to follow Your flight plan and to entrust the results to You. If You want me to tell my people, Your people, what has been happening in this cockpit, then help me know when, where, and how to do so. I really do not want to screw up again." With no "amen" or transition, Payne once more spoke directly to his wife. "Honey, I played the fool. I put my trust in a man I did not know and in a system tangled in the flesh. I chased the lie and rejected the truth."

Pastor Donovan did not let go of Ashley's hand. She did not say a word. Anne petted Bundt. After a minute or so of silence, Doug spoke: "What exactly is 'the truth'? I'm not trying to be Pilate here, nor am I trying to be funny. Dad, you're not the only one who's been thinking about all that's happened. 'Who really knows?' If you were to ask me that question, I would answer, 'George Carlson.' He seems to be in the know and have a say in everything. I find him a bit disturbing and freaky. He knew personal information about Anne that only she would know. How did he know it was the right time of the month for her to produce an egg for the procedure? To *me* (who lives with her) it seems like it's always that time of the month. So how did *he* know? And how did he know what her bedroom looked like? What was he plotting while he replicated it? He seems to control all that happens. I even wonder at times if he somehow caused mom's car accident in order to take her out of the picture for a while."

Pastor Donovan watched his son struggle and tense up after that last comment. Supposing Doug wrestled with whether or not he should have shared it, Payne (along with his ladies) could not have imagined the tension inside Doug nor anticipated what he intended to say next. Doug closed his eyes, lowered his head, and probed the unthinkable. "Do we *know* that the baby died? Did we *see* the baby? Or do we only have George's word? How do we know his true intentions?"

Anne immediately cross-examined her brother. "What are you saying, Doug? That he wanted my baby all to himself? That this was all a conspiracy to get Jesus for himself?"

"Anne, I'm only trying to be honest about what I've been thinking about as I've watered out in the backyard. And to be honest, it gets worse. What if George is a wolf in sheep's clothing? A false teacher who intends to not bring back Jesus, but rather the 'Anti-Jesus,' the counterfeit who looks like Jesus?"

"Now you're saying my baby is the Anti-Christ?"

"I'm just saying that we don't know what George is really up to. He's a mystery. As mom and dad stated earlier, 'Who really knows?'"

"Then let's find out," stated Anne with resolve, if not with anger in her voice.

"I have to agree," said Payne. He then turned to Ashley for final approval. "Let's find out."

He and the kids waited as she hesitated, as she undoubtedly calculated the ramifications of this decision. Squeezing her husband's hand, she concurred, "The truth *will* set us free."

The powwow concluded. The Donovans yoked together in agreement. They wanted answers, and they knew where they must go to get them.

* * * * *

Pastor Donovan called George Carlson the next morning. Ashley, Anne, and Doug listened on speakerphone. "Hello George, this is Pastor Donovan."

"I know. It's good to hear from you. I planned to go last Sunday to church to see how you were doing, but something came up. How is Anne?"

"She's recovering, doing okay under the circumstances. Her body is healing well. Actually, . . ."

"I'm glad to hear this," interjected George. "I know that you have some questions. If it works with your schedule, I would like for you and Anne to come by SarkiSystems next Monday night. I will answer your questions, as well as return to Anne the personal items she left behind, including the memorabilia and souvenirs she collected on her trip to Israel."

Pastor Donovan looked at Anne, then at Ashley. With their silent nod of approval, he responded, "That will be fine. You'll see us next Monday night at SarkiSystems." He deliberately said this last sentence to make sure that George and he and the others listening were on the same page.

"Actually, I'll see you and the whole family this coming Sunday morning at church. I have a surprise to show you."

With that announcement, the call ended. Huddled around the phone, the Donovans remained still. Undoubtedly doing what the others were doing, Payne quietly reflected on what would soon happen. *Am I ready for Sunday? What am I preaching on? What will it be like to go back to Sarki-Systems? Was George really glad to hear from us? What souvenirs? Did Anne bring back gifts for us? What is George's surprise? Did he bring back a gift?* All too familiar for Pastor Donovan, questions began to materialize and choke his spirit. This time, however, he resolved to find answers *and* not to look for them on his own.

* * * * *

The entire family arrived early to church on Sunday morning. Pastor Donovan knew this Lord's Day would be a difficult day. With his parishioners not seeing Anne for nearly half a year, he knew they would have lots of questions for her. With Anne not seeing George since her baby's death, he knew she would have lots of questions for him—even though her plan was to wait until Monday to confront him. Though he anticipated the day being difficult for Anne, the weight of his concern rested on Ashley. As he watched her timidly step out of the car and take calculated steps toward the sanctuary with trepidation, he thought, *How can I best protect her from the people, from George, from herself?* Walking with his Bible in one hand and his wife's hand in the other, he asked, "Would you like to help out in the nursery today?"

"No. I appreciate the offer to shield me, Payne, but I must face my fears . . . and my anger." Ashley held her husband's hand tightly as they entered the narthex.

Pastor Donovan preached with passion, and with not much guilt, the sermon he pulled from his file. The mystery of the incarnation, the embrace of both Jesus' humanity and deity presents a worthy topic for any Sunday, but especially for one during Advent. He concluded his message with this summary: "The One who was both 'revealed in the flesh' and 'vindicated in the Spirit' was and remains truly man and truly God. The One who was 'beheld by angels' and 'proclaimed among the nations' was and remains (to use what little Latin I know) *vera Deus* and *vera homo*, that is, truly God and truly man. The One who was 'believed on in the world' and 'taken up in glory' was and remains a mystery. The extent of His descent and ascent is incomprehensible. I may have earned a Master of Divinity degree, but that does not mean I have mastered the Divine. We cannot fully comprehend Him, but we can know Him. So let's get to know Him before it's too late. Let's learn to recognize His voice and follow Him—to His glory and our joy!"

Pastor Donovan felt good about the sermon, but more conspicuously, he emerged from the pulpit relieved, appearing free as he walked up the center isle to position himself to shake the people's hands. That is, until he spotted George in the back pew, previously concealed by the tall guests seated directly in front of him. He gave a pastoral smile to George and to the tall guests and to the lady next to George that he presumed also to be a guest. *'Tis the season for the Christmas and Easter Christians*, thought Pastor Donovan as he scanned the sanctuary to see where his family was and if they could see George. He greeted his parishioners, welcoming every compliment and comment—for each exchange delayed the reunion with George.

With postponement of the inevitable over, for only George and the visitor remained in the line, Pastor Donovan extended his hand and, with his pastoral voice, said, "It's good to see you. I hope you enjoyed the service."

"It's good to see you, too," said George while shaking hands. "I want to introduce you to Sister Rachel."

"Hello, and welcome. Is this your first time here? Or have we met before? You look familiar."

George answered for the guest. "*You* have not met her, but Anne has. They met in Israel." Before he could go into more detail, Anne, Ashley, and Doug approached the three of them. There, at the doors of the church, the six stood in a circle, reading each other's body language. Pastor Donovan paid close attention to Ashley's countenance. He knew first hand what she was capable of saying and how she could say it. He also observed Anne. Her stoic look, crossed arms, and clenched fists told him that her anger hid just below her skin.

Pointing to the young lady, Doug asked, "Who's this?"

"This is my surprise," stated George. "Anne, do you remember her?"

"I think so," responded Anne. Much to his relief, Pastor Donovan detected the volatility of this encounter lessen as his daughter's arms uncrossed and her voice held together. "But why is she here?"

"I will answer that and your other questions tomorrow night. But now I need to get her back to SarkiSystems, and you all need to go home and enjoy a 'world-famous' meal." George smiled; then he whisked Sister Rachel away and into the van awaiting them in the parking lot.

"So who was that, Anne?" asked Ashley as her eyes followed the van's exit off the church grounds.

"I believe she is one of the sisters that I met in Bethlehem."

"Why do you suppose she is here?"

"I have no idea, Mom. That is why I asked George."

"I have an idea," said Doug.

"I'm sure you do," said Anne, "but we're not interested in another one of your conspiracy theories."

Pastor Donovan used Anne's comment as a transition. "But we are interested in another Sunday lunch prepared by our own world-famous chef." The family groaned at his attempt to lighten the mood, but readily agreed. On the ride home, Payne conjured up a few theories of his own as to why the sister was there. Though unsure of the reason, he was fairly certain as to the how and the when of her advent—for he had watched that unforgettable plane fly overhead the other night.

*　*　*　*　*

Pastor Donovan and Anne arrived at SarkiSystems with their questions written down. Before they left home, the family laid hands on and prayed over the list, which included:

1. What did you do with the baby's body?

2. Are you sorry for what you did to Anne?

3. Do you still intend to carry out your plan?

4. Why did you fly the sister over from Israel?

5. How do you know it's Jesus' umbilical cord?

Censored off the list included questions too personal (Do you know what it's like to lose a child?) and too vindictive (Have you even read the Bible?). They sought answers, not an opportunity for spite.

"Welcome," said George Carlson. Pastor Donovan and Anne entered the all too familiar room as they would a lion's den. "I'm so glad you came. Please, have a seat." He motioned to the two chairs set up in front of him.

Anne asked her dad as they sat down, "Are we the only ones here tonight?"

"The team is busy at the moment," answered George who overheard, "but they hope to see you later when you pick up your belongings."

"Before Anne collects her stuff and we leave, we have a few questions that we want you to answer."

"I know."

"How do you know?" blurted Anne. She turned her head, raised her shoulders and her voice, "How does he always know?"

"I know you have questions because you told me at church yesterday that you had questions, and also because I see the piece of paper in your dad's shirt pocket that I assume has the questions listed down on it."

"You are right, once again," stated Payne as he reached into his shirt pocket with one hand and attempted to calm his daughter with the other. He read the five questions and then gave George the freedom to answer them in any order, but not the option to ignore even one.

"I thought you might have come with more questions."

"Oh, we could have come with many more questions," reacted Anne, even as her dad placed his arm around her. "Many more."

"I'll answer your questions in the order you asked them. First, we are in the process of cremating the body and plan to give you the ashes."

Pastor Donovan felt instant tension in Anne's body.

"I am sorry that you did not have the chance to see the baby. I'm sorry for all of us that this birth did not work. To answer your third question, yes, we are continuing the project—and this is why, to answer your fourth question, Sister Rachel is here."

"Wait," interjected Pastor Donovan. Staring at the list while holding firmly to his daughter, he submitted, "You flew her over here to authenticate the cord. That's your answer to our last question, isn't it?"

"Not exactly. She *can* vouch for the cord, but her mission here goes beyond that. And *that* is the surprise I want to show you."

With those words said, a young man in a white coat entered the room from the side door leading to Anne's "bedroom" and where the procedure took place. Pastor Donovan now needed both hands to keep Anne from falling to the floor. In truth, like a Roman arch, they kept each other up as crippling fear, guilt, and anger entered through the opened door.

"I want to introduce Barry. He is a pre-med major (first in his class!) and our newest intern here at SarkiSystems. He's going to take you inside while I take care of some unfinished business." George gestured for Barry to come assist Pastor Donovan and Anne, and then walked out the door leading to the parking lot.

"Are you okay?" asked Barry. "You obviously are troubled about something. Is there anything I can do for you before I take you to the back?"

"Just give us a minute. This is not easy for us, especially for my daughter. The memories are too fresh and painful, but she's determined to face them."

"Did something happen to her?" asked the new intern.

"You don't know?"

"No. Last week was my first week working here. I've been helping out with the experiments in the lab and taking care of the new girl. I haven't been in on the meetings Mr. Carlson holds with his team."

"They have not told you about my baby?" asked Anne, stressing each word as she lifted her inflamed eyes to observe Barry for the first time.

"That is your baby?"

Before Barry continued, Anne probed, "You've seen my baby?"

"I don't know, but I have been working with . . ." Barry stopped midsentence, then stated, "I'm supposed to escort the two of you to the boardroom inside." Then, he waited, not impatiently, but attentively like a waiter ready to serve and assist those sitting at a table. "Are you ready? It's not too far of a walk; just down a hallway and before the lab."

"I know where it is," asserted Anne as she stood up. "It's at the end of the hall, sandwiched between my mock 'bedroom' and 'the den of robbers,' the inner chamber where the team works its magic and where you now work."

Though not adopting Anne's tone, Pastor Donovan concurred with his daughter's description. Questions bombarded him as the three stood and turned toward the open door. *Is she ready? Will this help her heal? What unfinished business does George have to attend to? What is Barry the new guy working on? Is he going to work on Anne?* Determined not to mess up this time, he grabbed Anne's hand, and together they walked through the door. He was not about to watch her walk alone through that door and into that hallway where the team whisked her away to be impregnated and where he heard the cries of her childbirth but never her child.

"Welcome to the hallway of darkness and ignorance," announced Anne under her breath so only her dad could hear. Barry led the way to the boardroom. Each step down the hall reminded Pastor Donovan of his foolishness and the reason for Anne's anger. The picture of the reliquary on the wall, the smell of medical experiments in the air, and, of course, the bedroom up ahead prompted him once again to doubt his worthiness as a father, husband, and pastor. *What was I thinking? Why did I not seek advice? How could I have been so deceived? What on earth was I doing?*

Before disbelief thoroughly choked him, Anne let go of his hand and headed toward her old bedroom. Barry quickly intercepted her, shut the door, and said, "That door was supposed to be shut." Pastor Donovan could tell Barry was disturbed; that he was the intern who wanted to follow instructions and make a good impression. Motioning to the next door down the hallway, Barry instructed his two responsibilities, "Mr. Carlson wants both of you in the boardroom. He will join you momentarily. Until then, make yourself comfortable."

Just before they entered the room, a gentleman in a white coat swung open the door to the adjacent laboratory and revealed before the intern could stop him, "Barry, the liver analysis is complete. The specimen is ready to be destroyed." Pastor Donovan sensed more uneasiness in the intern as he scurried them into the room and closed the door. Payne and Anne both stiffened temporarily when they heard the door lock.

"Dad?"

"I know, Precious." Pastor Donovan looked at Anne and then scanned the room. A conference table surrounded by executive chairs occupied most of the space. A white board covered an entire wall and a video projector hung from the ceiling. "Let's just get your things and get out of here."

"Dad," whispered Anne as she sat down and invited her dad to do the same. She leaned in so he could hear her soft voice, "I saw inside the rooms. As if everything but my focus moved in slow motion, I spotted things beyond what real time would allow."

"Why are you whispering?"

"Because he may be listening." Anne pointed to the flower centerpiece on the table and the projector up above. She made him face her so he could read her lips. "I know what's happening. I know the answers to our questions. I know the surprise." Shifting in his seat and tilting his good ear toward Anne, Pastor Donovan readied himself for the unveiling. "Dad, the sister is over here to . . ." Anne's mouth shut and her eyes widened as the door to the boardroom opened.

"Why?" asked Pastor Donovan, unaware that they were not alone. "Why is she here?"

"I'll explain and clarify that in just a few minutes," replied George as he and Sister Rachel walked into the room. "But first, I want to show you all a short video." Once the sister sat down, George turned off the lights and turned on the projector.

The video documented the current state of the world—the rise in wars and rumors of wars, earthquakes and weather-caused disasters, along with the collapse of governments and economies, human morality and civility. The images and narration moved Pastor Donovan to wonder, *How much longer can the world go on like this? Who will God raise up to lead us out of this mess? Or, more likely, when will God say 'Enough is enough' and send His Son to judge the living and the dead?*

George turned the lights back on and announced with an air of pride, "I call this video 'Demand.' The three of you in this room are aware of the 'supply' that we have, or, more accurately, will have soon."

"You've lost me, George," declared Pastor Donovan.

"The plan to usher in the Day of the Lord and set up God's kingdom involves two concurrent projects: supply and demand. We supply the return of Jesus *and* the demand for His return. You are an integral part of SarkiSystem's 'supply' division; but there is an entire 'demand' division that eluded you until tonight." George lifted up the blank white board on the wall, exposing another board behind it with the following three lines written on it:

Lewis Barnone

Virtual and Viral

Ideas and Vision

George faced the three in the room and explained, "The narrator you heard on the video is named Lewis Barnone. He is not real. Our 'demand' team created him. Over this past year he has gained much notoriety and influence; but, over the next nine months, we project that everybody in the world *will* get to know him. 'He' will gain tremendous power and influence by infiltrating government and banking systems. Lewis Barnone will become a world leader who defines the new era and offers global solutions."

"He sounds like the Anti-Christ," remarked Pastor Donovan.

"He *is* the Anti-Christ."

"This is all ludicrous," stated Anne. "It's absurd to think that you want us to believe that you have created the Anti-Christ."

"What's absurd is to think that the Anti-Christ is some person—a president, a pope, some celebrity. He's not human. He's virtual. He's digital, not physical. How else can he appear omniscient and omnipresent? Lewis

Barnone is set to enter into six billion personal lives with authority—and this is only possible through the infinite ones and zeros of technology. He (I mean, we) will influence, market, and ultimately control peoples' ideas and vision of reality through such means as social media, television, computers, smart phones, and videos like the one you just watched. Who could have ever dreamed that satellites, cell towers, and microchips would incite people to want a Savior to come? These are exciting times."

"I can't believe I'm a part of this," muttered Anne cynically.

"Actually, Anne, your part is done. Which brings me to the surprise and why Sister Rachel is here."

"I know why she is here," stated Anne. "I saw her room."

"You do? You did?" asked George. For the first time Pastor Donovan sensed George to be baffled, a bit off his game plan. He also sensed Anne to be on the offense. Like watching an ultimate fighter unleash a flurry of assaults, he sat in his ringside executive chair mesmerized and amazed at his daughter's intuition and intensity.

"She is here to carry your 'supply' and continue your plan," stated Anne. "You have done to her what you did to me. You even made up her room to look like the sisters' underground chamber in Bethlehem. Do you really think this will feel like home to her?"

Allowing no time for George to respond, Anne turned and addressed Sister Rachel. "Have they performed the procedure on you?" The girl simply dropped her head and folded her hands onto the table. Watching this sister's head and hands shake with shame, Anne turned back to George. "How could you? Didn't you learn anything from me?"

"We did learn from you and continue to learn from the baby," interjected George. "You have provided invaluable data. Thank you; but it's time to press on. With more research and development we determined that Sister Rachel, because of her fidelity and proximity to the cord, makes a more suitable carrier for Jesus. So, to answer your question, yes, we successfully implanted the embryo with Jesus' cells into her last week. Everything is now in place. In nine months the entire world will be ready for our Lord's return."

"And Sister Rachel will deliver," snapped Anne. "You've got it all figured out. Supply and demand: it's that simple. It's a good thing God has you working for Him. What would He do without SarkiSystems?"

Anne stood up, looked at the white board, and said, "Dad, it's fool-proof. Like the tire shop owner we heard about who dropped nails in the road in order to watch profits inflate, George has released 'Lewis Barnone' to create and market the need. Farfetched? Some may think so, but the masses will demand a divine intervention and SarkiSystems will be there to supply it. Thank you, George, for exposing your vision. It's clear and ambitious."

Pastor Donovan stood up as Anne attended his chair like a gentleman would his date, and as she shared her departing words. "We must go now. We'll collect my belongings (I know where they are) and show ourselves out (we know the way)." As she opened the door, she turned and directly faced George. "One more thing: do let me know when Barry the intern and the others in the lab are done dissecting my baby. I would like his remains after you've fully studied and cremated him."

Though nothing was said as they walked out, Pastor Donovan heard volumes in the trembling silence of the two who remained in the boardroom. He liked what he heard.

* * * * *

Pastor Donovan smiled when he saw Ashley, Doug, and Bundt come out the front door when Anne and he pulled into the driveway. "They really do want to know how it went tonight."

"I think Doug is more interested in what I bought for him in Israel," said Anne. They shared a smile and then a deep breath as they got out of the car.

Payne carried the box of Anne's belongings into the house. The family filed in after him like eager students entering their classroom on the first day of class. They sat ready, if not impatient in the living room for the report to begin.

"Did you get answers from that man?" asked Ashley.

"Yes, but I think I got more insight from Anne. You would have been proud of her. She flustered George with her sensing and sarcasm. She zoned in on his vision, intentions, and means."

"You go, girl," said Doug with his hand raised and ready to give a high-five to his sister. "So how diabolical is 'that man'? What can you tell us?"

"I can tell you everything," answered Anne. Though she did not high-five her brother, she did sit up straight to elucidate. "It's full speed ahead for SarkiSystems. They are convinced that the umbilical cord is in fact Jesus' and that they can use it for God's purposes. They have brought Sister Rachel here to carry baby Jesus, though I am not sure that is why she is here. They have already impregnated her and plan to . . ."

"What?" gasped Ashley. "They did to her what they did to you?"

"Not only did they, but, again, I'm not convinced this is what she wants. She looks scared, lost, and ashamed. Whereas, George looks confident that he's got the right girl now for the job. He learned from me and from my baby—which brings me to something that I know will hit me hard when I have time to reflect on it. Mom . . ." Anne suddenly paused. Without warning, the time to reflect was at hand. As she fought back tears that impeded her vision and speech, she gestured "stop" to her father so that he would not make any effort to take over the reporting of what happened. Payne and the rest of the family respected her instruction.

Anne composed herself and reveled, "Mom, they have been doing experiments on Joshua. They are examining his body piece-by-piece, learning all they can under their microscopes in their lab. When they are done with a part, they systematically cremate it. And when they are all done, they will hand me his ashes."

"This man and all his technicians should be arrested and put away for a long, *long* time," asserted Ashley. "I mean it. What they are doing there at that place is wrong. It's evil and illegal."

"Mom, I'm not done."

"But wait, there's more!" announced Doug in his best infomercial voice.

"Doug, you'll like this," said Anne. "George is preparing the way for the Lord by creating the Anti-Christ. He's controlling the supply and demand for the second coming."

"This man's not just criminal; he's psychotic," snapped Ashley.

Payne reached out to Ashley with his hand and heart. "You're right, Honey. And I am so sorry I dragged us into all this." He wanted then to say, "We must stop him," but instead he just held his wife's hand. He resolved not to pull his family into another plan without consulting them and Scripture. He sat quietly with his thoughts and prayers. *I do think my ladies will want to stop George. I know Doug will welcome the adventure. And Lord, I do think You want us to rescue Sister Rachel and to shut down SarkiSystems.* As he sat in the living room holding Ashley's hand, he heard a voice say, "But wait, there's more." He turned to smile at Doug, but he was not there, and neither was Anne. Evidently the powwow concluded while he remained contemplative on the couch. Now present and aware, he could hear Anne and Doug playing in the kitchen with the gift she brought back for him from Israel. He could also hear his wife's trust growing as they sat alone in the living room. He knew this would be vital as they faced God's "But wait, there's more."

8

MUCH TO PASTOR DONOVAN'S delight, the remaining season of Advent went according to schedule. People responded well to his sermons. Anne's body recovered well from the delivery. The Donovans enjoyed their Christmas Eve tradition of taking their fine china, silverware, crystal glasses, candles, and linen tablecloth to the local fast food restaurant. Though Pastor Donovan protects the week between Christmas and New Year's for vacation, it does not always work out according to plan. But this year, even though they did not go anywhere, he successfully set aside the entire week for family time.

During this "staycation" the family enjoyed playing games, watching old movies, and eating lots of food—and doing so together. From the kitchen, Payne could watch Doug water the olive tree, hear Anne talk to Bundt in her room, and taste test Ashley's latest world-famous meal. He could also ponder if God was giving him another special message for the church as it entered a new year.

Over the years the congregation has learned to listen to and heed his word. It all started the year he sensed God saying "This year free and clear" regarding the mortgage on the church. The people politely attributed this idea to a young pastor's high hopes; that is, until the end of the year when the church celebrated the burning of the mortgage. A few years later he sensed, after reading the thirty-second Psalm, that God was asking him to pray for God's heavy hand to be placed on the congregation like it had been on King David. He told the people that there was hidden sin in the camp and that it must be dealt with in order for the church to move forward. Though the people did not like what he said, they did concede his credibility. Following a hard year of dealing with a church leader being convicted of a felony crime, two married members confessing to having an affair, and a youth volunteer having inappropriate contact with those under his care, the church felt a fresh movement of God's Spirit and a freedom unlike anything they had experienced before.

Determined not to manufacture a word from the Lord or insist on one, Pastor Donovan waited patiently to hear from God. Whether in the kitchen, in the backyard, standing, sitting, or lying down, he considered throughout the week what God might want to reveal. He prayed without ceasing, *Do You have a special word for my people? What do You want to say to us as we begin another year?* On New Year's Eve, as the family gathered at the dinner table to enjoy a filet mignon-baked potato-Caesar salad-chocolate pie dinner, Payne asked, "Whose turn is it to say the blessing?" At that moment a word, literally *a* word came to him: *Blessing!* He heard God's still small voice say, "It's your turn, pastor. I want you to pronounce a blessing upon and be a blessing to your people and to Me."

Staring at the steak in front of him, Doug eagerly asked, "So, Dad, whose turn is it?"

"Evidently it's my turn," remarked Payne. Then, with a consenting smile, he reiterated, "Yes, it's my turn to bring the blessing."

After the blessing, the Donovans enjoyed a delicious meal and welcomed in a new year. As they each headed for bed, Pastor Donovan wondered, *What does this year have in store? What kind of a year will this be?* As he placed his head on the pillow and his left arm around Ashley, he heard the word once again, "Blessing." *How ironic,* he thought, *I sought a word for my people but instead found a word for myself.*

* * * * *

Though it was a word for him, Pastor Donovan understood that it was a word to share with his people. So, on the first Sunday of January, with a congregation primed for a special message, he preached on *blessing.* He shared with them that he was going to be intentional about blessing them, of projecting good into their lives. He explained to them that the English word "eulogy" comes from the Greek word "*eulogia*" meaning "to speak well of." He asked, "Why do we give eulogies only at funerals? Why not eulogize the living? Why do we wait until after people die to 'speak well of' them?"

The text for the sermon was Numbers 6:24–26, the well-known priestly blessing that pronounces:

The Lord bless you, and keep you;

The Lord make His face shine on you, and be gracious to you;

The Lord lift up His countenance on you, and give you peace.

Pastor Donovan expounded on each line, presenting the depth of each phrase. He summed up the meaning of this blessing by giving his own paraphrase: "May the Lord bring good to you, protect you, and see you flourish. May the full blaze of His love and grace enlighten, comfort, empower, and forgive you. May He look right at you and smile, and bring you well-being and wholeness."

He concluded the message by telling his people that he intended to visit each one of them in their homes over the course of the year. "I believe God wants me to do three things at these house blessings. First, He wants me to *invoke* His presence into your house. Second, He wants me to *intercede* for your well-being and the well-being of your family and friends. And third, He wants me to *inspire* you in your spiritual journey, helping you see how He is writing His story on the pages of your life."

Being the first Sunday of the month, not just of the year, the service concluded with the congregation celebrating the Lord's Supper. Following the bread and the cup and the singing of the closing hymn, Pastor Donovan stood at the back door ready to shake hands and to offer a brief but sincere blessing to each member and guest.

"Must feel good, Pastor, to hit a homerun on your first at bat of the new season," announced Brother Bob.

"Thank you for being a team player, Bob." With a grin, Pastor Donovan continued, "I look forward to 'fielding' your questions, as well as 'batting' around ideas and touching 'base' with you when I come to visit you."

Much to Pastor Donovan's surprise, more than one parishioner expressed concern, even panic, about these upcoming house blessings. "Pastor, you will call before you come, right? I'm not always dressed appropriately, if you know what I mean." "Do you have to come into my house? To be honest, Pastor, I'm embarrassed and ashamed of what it looks like." Pastor Donovan greeted each uneasiness with a listening ear and a reassuring smile.

This feels right, he thought as he shook his parishioners' hands. *This is the perfect way to start the new year. Thank you, God, for giving me a word.* But then, with one simple glance to see how many remained in line, Pastor Donovan's thoughts scattered. *No. No. This is all wrong. Why, Lord? How could You do this to me? This is* not *the way I want to start off the year.*

At the end of the line stood George Carlson—an approaching dark cloud ready to unleash a flurry of charms and distractions. *Lord, I'm not sure I can bless him. I'm not sure I should bless him.*

"That was an apt message," stated George as he stretched out his hand. "It's as if you read my mind and prepared the way for my being here."

"I'm glad you liked it," responded Pastor Donovan with puzzlement masked in poise. "It sounds like you received a blessing."

"I did," replied George, "but I'm here to ask if Anne would come visit Sister Rachel and bring a blessing to her. She's been having a difficult time with the pregnancy and has requested to see Anne, *the* one person who understands and can relate to what she is going through. Truth is, Payne, she could really use a friend right now; for, along with morning sickness, I believe she is dealing with homesickness. I believe the word that God gave to you is for Anne, too. Just as your people will benefit from your visits, so Sister Rachel will benefit from a 'home blessing' by Anne."

"Obviously, I will need to talk with Anne and to Ashley about this."

"Of course," reacted George with a touch of impatience. "I will call you tomorrow. But just know, she could really use a blessing as soon as possible."

"Better yet, I will call you," insisted Payne. "You'll hear from me as soon as we make our decision. Until then, may the Lord bless her and keep her."

With this said, George parted for the parking lot. Pastor Donovan remained at the doors of the church and probed his blessing. *Why did I say, 'The Lord bless her and keep her,' and not, 'The Lord bless you and keep you'? Can I ever become the kind of person who could bless George?* Unsure how to answer his own questions, Pastor Donovan headed to the office to rendezvous with the ones who could help him discern and discover. He knew his family would be in his study because they made a New Year's resolution to meet there after the service to pray for God's blessing on his morning's message and on his preparations for the next week's sermon.

* * * * *

"Honey, is there something on your mind?" asked Ashley. "You have been rather quiet—in the office, in the car, and now at lunch. Is everything alright?"

Pastor Donovan may have been quiet, but he was speaking, carrying on a candid exchange with God ever since George turned to go to his car. *Do*

I limit a blessing? This question kept coming up in his mind. He was unclear, though, as to who was asking it. Was he? God? Both? The interchange of the prayer remained fervent, an open dialogue between two fathers. *What do you want me to do?* Faced with another question without a clear supplicant, yet one with pressing weight, Pastor Donovan remained quiet. That is, until Doug announced that he saw George Carlson sitting in church.

A collective "What?" came forth from Ashley and Anne.

Dropping her fork onto her plate, Ashley inquired, "Is this true, Payne?"

"Yes, George was at church and, yes, that is why I have been rather quiet. And, no, everything is not alright." With this terse set of answers, Payne stood up from the table and divulged, "We need to talk about a favor he is asking of us—well, actually, of Anne."

"Sounds like a powwow to me," said Doug. "When and where do you want us to meet?"

"I'd like it to be now because I will not be able to think about anything else until we make a decision. And I'd like to do it out on the back porch because I could use the fresh air."

Like a piper, Pastor Donovan led an entranced family out the back door. Wasting no time, while the four of them dusted off the patio chairs, he prayed, "May God grant us wisdom and clarity and strength to do the right thing at the right time for the right reason." Still standing, but not standing still, he divulged the request and their dilemma. "Sister Rachel wants Anne to visit her. Evidently she is having pregnancy problems and wants to talk to . . ."

"Already?" interrupted Ashley. "It's only been a little over a month. What problems could she possibly have at this stage?"

"I'm not exactly sure, but George said something about morning sickness and homesickness."

"I think it's more than that," said Anne. "I've been praying for her ever since I saw her at SarkiSystems. I have this feeling, call it a mother's intuition, that she is reaching out for more than a friend."

A mother's intuition? How can she have a . . . Payne abruptly withdrew his reflection as he took his seat, a seat that faced him directly toward the olive tree. Flabbergasted and ashamed by his insensitivity, yet relieved that it remained unsaid, he repositioned himself. This adjustment procured him time to refocus, both on his family and on the matter at hand. "What should we do? George wants Anne to be a blessing to Sister Rachel. The question, though, is, do *we* want Anne to be a blessing?"

"No, Dad," remarked Anne. "The question is, do *I* want to be a blessing to her?"

"Well, actually," corrected Doug, "shouldn't the question be, does *God* want Anne to be a blessing to Sister Rachel?"

"Well, I can't speak for God or for Anne, but I can speak for myself," asserted Ashley. "And I say let someone else be a blessing." With this verdict, she shifted in her seat. Payne watched his wife's countenance become unsettled as *she* now faced the olive tree. "There must be someone else who can help this young girl. Surely there is someone who can identify with this girl," maintained Ashley, and then paused before continuing, "someone who can identify with this vulnerable, lonely, scared girl who has been taken advantage of by this evil man."

"Mom, you know I am that 'someone' whom you speak of." Anne's prophetic-like announcement produced a hush on the patio, stillness conducive for a library housing stacks of reflections.

"No, please, no," cried Ashley.

Unsure whom she implored—*Is she begging Anne, George, Sister Rachel, God, me?*—Payne chose to keep his mouth shut. *I will not play the fool this time.*

"Mom," reassured Anne, "I too want nothing more to do with that man. But that girl, she wants our help. She needs our help. Whatever she thought she was going to do over here away from her order is not what has happened."

"She's out of her boat, in a storm, in over her head, and calling out, 'Anne, save me.'" Doug's use of the Apostle Peter's sinking-in-the-storm incident helped the family to collectively assess Sister Rachel's predicament.

"And like Jesus, I'm supposed to reach out to her," said Anne. "I'm the one best positioned to . . ."

"Be a blessing," interjected Payne. Though one of his top pet peeves is people finishing his sentences, he could not hold back his thought.

"Why does she have to be the one?" asked Ashley, now with consideration. "How come she is the only one?"

Is she the only one? Were there others before Anne? Is she in a long line of surrogate Marys? Are there others that George could have approached to help? Did he ask the others and they refused? Questions flashed inside Pastor Donovan, but then vanished when Ashley and Anne stood up, embraced, and stared with tear-filled eyes at the olive tree. Joining them, he announced, "If Anne goes, I go. I do not trust that man."

"Oh you of little faith," smirked Doug as he joined the group hug.

There, on the patio, the Donovans stood united. Anne will visit Sister Rachel. Payne will accompany Anne. No one will trust George.

* * * * *

Pastor Donovan called George in the morning to inform him that Anne *and* he will come visit Sister Rachel. He felt empowered deciding the course of action. Even while driving to SarkiSystems that evening, he felt like he was in the driver's seat, and with Anne riding shotgun, they would together change the course of the supply and demand. They were on a mission—a mission not just to encourage Sister Rachel, but to rescue her.

"Thank you for coming with such short notice," said George Carlson as he greeted Pastor Donovan and Anne in the parking lot. "Sister Rachel welcomed the news of your coming with a smile. The last time I saw her smile was over a month ago when she first saw the reliquary."

Pastor Donovan and Anne said nothing as they entered the building, as though instinctively aware that they were being watched and recorded. While two chairs loomed ready in the infamous gathering room, they both stood, a sly but straightforward gesture of control.

"Please, have a seat," said George.

"We'd rather stand," replied Pastor Donovan. "We are eager to bring a blessing to Sister Rachel."

"There is one thing we need to talk about before the visit."

"Then maybe *you* should take a seat," suggested Anne with a straight face.

"That won't be necessary," countered George in a perturbed tone. "Because the sister requested only to see Anne, only Anne can go in to see her. But Payne, you can stay here while the two of them visit."

Pastor Donovan and Anne glanced at each other, just making sure that they were on the same page of the Donovan playbook. "That is unacceptable, George," said Payne. "I specifically told you that we both would come visit her. That is what Anne wants. It is what I want. And it is what Ashley and Doug want." Motioning to the two separate doors in the room, he continued, "Either I walk in through that door with Anne or she and I will walk out though that door and go home."

Pastor Donovan observed George consider the ultimatum. Then he observed the intern enter the room. "Barry, please escort these two inside," instructed George. "And, Payne, to honor the sister's request and to satisfy yours, would you be willing to sit right outside the bedroom to begin with? And if Sister Rachel opts to have you visit her too, then you can join them. Is *that* acceptable?"

Again, Pastor Donovan and Anne glanced at each other. Anne nodded, serving as the Donovan family spokesperson. With Barry leading the way, they entered the hallway and headed directly to the refurbished bedroom.

"Please wait here," said Barry to Pastor Donovan. "I'll get you a chair in just a moment."

"I'll be okay, Dad," said Anne as Barry opened the door to Sister Rachel's room.

Pastor Donovan prayed silently there in the hallway, the hallway that showcased framed photos of the "supply" and doors leading to the infamous laboratory and to the boardroom where he was introduced to the "demand." With the reminders pressing in around him of the dark passage traveled over the past year, he disciplined himself to count his many blessings. *Thank You, God, for not leaving us or forsaking us. Thank You that we can now be here to help this young girl. Please give us wisdom and strength to discern what is really going on. May You open the door for us to be a blessing. We want to be instruments in Your hands that . . .*

"Here," announced Barry as he placed the chair down, clueless that he was interrupting prayer.

"Thank you," said Pastor Donovan. Then, for some unforeseen reason—maybe to pass the time away—he asked, "Barry, do you pray?"

"All the time," answered the intern. "Ever since I was a little boy I have talked with God. Why do you ask?" Following an awkward moment of silence, Barry continued, "I assume you do. You're a pastor. In fact, you were probably just praying. You were just praying, weren't you? I just disturbed a pastor praying. I'm so, so sorry."

"It's okay," assured Pastor Donovan. "It's not the unpardonable sin. God understands and so do I." They exchanged smiles, but then they shared concern as Anne exited the room with urgency in her eyes.

"We need to go," asserted Anne. "Sister Rachel needs her rest."

"Already?" asked Payne with confusion. "Did she say I could go in to see her?"

"Now, Dad," insisted Anne.

Questions accompanied Pastor Donovan as Anne and he power walked in silence out to the car. *Are we abandoning the mission? Is she saying, "Mission accomplished; let's get out of here"? Are we in danger? What's happening?*

Only after both car doors shut did Anne speak. "Dad, she slipped me a note as we sat on her bed. I thought she just wanted to hold my hand, just wanted to reach out for some comfort and reassurance." Anne hesitated to divulge anything more until the car turned out of the parking lot and off the property of SarkiSystems. "Dad, the note says, 'Please get me and the blessed cord out of here.'"

"Then why are we here in the car and not in her room plotting how we can bring about her wish?" asked Payne.

"Because when I looked at her after reading the note, she whispered with trembling lips, "If they catch you with this they will not let you come back." She then glanced at a ceiling camera, confident that I understood that someone would soon be coming to check on us. "Dad, I squeezed her hand, reassuring her that I did understand. As I stood up, she said to me and to anyone listening in, "I'm sorry you cannot stay longer. Please come back. I'll be right here awaiting your next visit; it's not like I have plans to go anywhere else."

Anne stared at the note for the rest of the drive home. Pastor Donovan stared straight ahead at the road, and yet he remained focused on those ten words that would define *blessing*: "Please get me and the blessed cord out of here."

* * * * *

"Why are you home so soon?" asked Ashley.

The confused look on her face as she stood on the front porch reminded Payne that the visit had been a family affair. Doug's hope-laden yet naive "Is she in the car?" question reminded Payne that there was much work to be done. As he answered his son with "No, she is not in the car," Pastor Donovan thought to himself, *Obviously he needs a reality check.* And as he entered the house and shared with Ashley the basic facts of the visit, he thought, *What we really need here is a plan, a plan forged in wisdom and fortitude.*

"May I see the note?" asked Ashley as the four Donovan's sat in the living room for an impromptu powwow.

Payne watched in wonder as his wife coddled the note. Her careful handling of the paper and her attention to every word brought tears to her eyes and an awareness to his mind: *I have not actually seen the note.*

Allowing a healthy amount of time for her to sit with the message, he asked, "May I see the note?" He immediately felt a connection to Sister Rachel, as if the note became some kind of portal, when Ashley handed him the piece of paper.

"She's in trouble. She needs our help." Pastor Donovan spoke these words with urgency—as if he were hearing her cry for help in real time, as if, at that very moment, he were seeing her in agony and pain.

"Dad, that's what I've been saying. She is in way over her head. She came here to rescue the cord. Getting pregnant was not part of the plan." Anne hesitated, and then qualified, "At least not part of the original plan."

"I don't understand," admitted Doug.

"In desperation, Sister Rachel must have believed that the only way to get what she wanted was to do what George wanted. I think she thought that she could win his favor and persuade him to give back the cord."

"Or at least buy her time to come up with a plan," offered Ashley.

"So the pregnancy *was* planned," surmised Doug.

"It was Plan B," clarified Anne. "A planned, but unwanted pregnancy."

Though still enchanted by the note, Pastor Donovan heard every word his family exchanged. As if speaking directly to the sister through the paper in his hand, he interjected, "It was Plan B for George, too. Anne, my daughter, was Plan A. And now, Sister Rachel, you are Plan B." Immediately having said this, Pastor Donovan realized that he, and not just Doug, needed a reality check. He shifted his eyes away from what was in his hands and onto what was there beside him: a family in need of help and a family that needs to help.

The living room became quiet—maybe because they all needed sleep after such a long day, or maybe because Plan B had started and they needed time to process what actually was at hand. For whatever reason or combination of reasons, the four sat still for a while. And for a while Payne welcomed the stillness. The silence proved fortifying, not awkward. It provided him space to pray. *The sister really is in trouble. She needs our help. She needs* Your *help. We* need *Your help. Please, guide our steps. Open and close doors as You wish, but please give us wisdom and strength to discern and do what You wish. We don't want Plan A, Plan B, or Plan C. We want* Your *plan. We want Thy plan to be done on earth as . . .*

"Bundt killed a cat early this morning," announced Anne, breaking the silence and her father's prayer-filled concentration.

"Did you see it happen?" asked Doug.

"Yes."

"Cool."

"Not cool," snapped Anne. "He woke me up because he needed to go outside. When I opened the back door, he dashed out and cornered the cat by the back fence. I tried to stop him but his hunter instincts were in full operation. Bundt neutralized the cat's every move as he closed in. As a last-ditch effort, the cat leaped into the corner bush. Bundt immediately went right in after her. And, just like in a cartoon, the bush shook back and forth and then threw them out. That's when Bundt went in for the kill. With the cat firmly in his jaws, he shook her back and forth and then spit her out to lie dead on the lawn. Standing tall with his chest puffed out, he strode right over his kill, right past the olive tree, straight into the house, and fixed himself right at *this* window where he stared outside surveying his kingdom."

As Anne pointed directly at the front window there in the living room where the powwow was taking place, Pastor Donovan could not help but think that this animalistic incident was a parable of Plans A and B. *Bundt is George and Anne is the cat.* Although perceiving residual anger or perchance determination in Anne's voice and motion, he immediately reinterpreted. *Anne is Bundt and George is the cat.* Unsure what to think and confused as to why Anne even recounted the pre-dawn clash, Payne sat dumbstruck, and gazed out the window like the rest of his family.

Then, with her own hunter instinct, Anne erupted. "He will trespass no more. Not on my watch. Not in my backyard."

"He?" queried Doug, seeking clarification.

"George," snapped Anne rather melodramatically. "We must stop him. Expose his lies. Put an end to his ways. Call it revenge. Call it justice. I don't care what you call it. My sister will give birth to her baby, not his 'supply.' Soon, very soon, she will be free and he will not. And she will come live with us until she is ready to return home. As for George, as far as I'm concerned, he can go straight to . . ."

"Anne!" exclaimed Ashley. "You are right. And we stand together on seeing that Sister Rachel is rescued and that that man is sentenced and put away for a long time."

"A very long time," barked Anne as she stared out the window, looking ready to execute the judgment.

Though Payne knew that the family knew that more should and would be said about how to proceed forward with God's plan, he also knew that they knew that they all were tired and that a good night's sleep and a few days of reflection and prayer and cooling off would be both welcomed and useful. As they headed for bed, Pastor Donovan stopped at each room and prayed a blessing. When he placed his head on his pillow and his arm around his wife, he prayed softly so that both God and Ashley would hear. "Heavenly Father, thank You for my family. Bless us as we seek to be a blessing. We want to be right in what we do, and we want to be good as we do it. Good night."

9

"Why not just ask him to let her go?" suggested Doug at the breakfast table.

"That man will never give her up," reacted Ashley as she scrambled eggs. "He will never give up. Never admit he is wrong. He will just come up with new plans until he gets it right. But he will never get it right. He's deluded. He's deranged. That man will not let Sister Rachel go until she is no longer of any more use to him."

"Honey, I think the eggs are ready," interjected Payne. Watching Ashley beat the eggs in the frying pan while answering their son's simplistic suggestion confirmed Payne's hunch that one night's sleep had not provided enough time to process the situation or to make any decision.

"Then what *do* we do?" asked Doug.

"I think Anne and I should visit Sister Rachel again," answered Payne. "She needs to know that we are here to help her, that her note did not land on deaf ears."

"Do you think Anne is up for that?" asked Ashley.

Perceiving that the question projected his wife's own apprehension and fear, Payne reassured her, "I don't think we could stop her. She's all in on rescuing Sister Rachel, or as she referred to her last night, 'my sister.' Honey, she is definitely up for it."

"She may be up for 'it,' but she is not up for breakfast," said Doug rather snidely. "Where is she? I'm hungry. Can we eat without her? Whose turn is it to pray?"

"I think she and Bundt are still asleep," said Ashley, "probably making up for yesterday's early morning ordeal."

"So, yes, Doug, we can eat without her. And it's your turn," declared Payne; then he said with a smile, "And make it short. I'm hungry, too."

* * * * *

The family's consensus waxed as the week waned. There arose agreement and no compromise. Pastor Donovan and Anne would return to Sarki-Systems to visit Sister Rachel. They would go deliver a blessing, but they would also go as scouts on a reconnaissance mission to gather information—for they were convinced that blessing Sister Rachel meant rescuing Sister Rachel.

Pastor Donovan called George to arrange the visit. Due to "travel plans" (George would not disclose any further details), the meeting would have to wait until the second Monday of February. This ill-timed, one-month excursion forced the Donovans to postpone their operation. Though not ignored, this elephant in the house laid low as the four of them attempted to return to everyday life. Doug worked on raising his grades. Anne worked on friendships that had lapsed during her gap year. Ashley worked on cleaning the house and cooking new dishes. Payne worked on blessing his parishioners and his wife.

With football season over and Valentine's Day just around the corner, the second visit was at hand. The day did not sneak up on them for Doug faithfully marked off the days on the calendar. At every meal they could stare at the countdown as it hung on the kitchen wall.

"Should you call to confirm that you are going tonight?" asked Ashley.

"That won't be necessary. George knows we're coming," answered Anne, even though her mom directed the question to her dad. "He's always in the know."

After a family prayer out by the car, Pastor Donovan and Anne drove down the street like soldiers off to war, instruments of righteousness.

Barry the intern stood under a light pole in the parking lot ready to greet them. "You know, Dad, he's kinda cute," remarked Anne as they drove right up to him. This observation befuddled Pastor Donovan. *Where did that come from? Is this her way of relieving stress? Is she nervous? Does she think I'm nervous? When did my little girl start noticing boys?* As puzzling as his daughter's comment was, the fact that Barry, not George, stood ready to welcome them disturbed him more.

Choosing neither to reply to Anne's quip nor to conjecture as to why the intern and not the mastermind stood before them, Pastor Donovan simply smiled as he got out of the car. "Good evening, Barry. You look good. How do you stay in such good shape while working here and going to school?" He sported a big grin while his daughter veiled a blushing face. Pastor Donovan did not hear Barry's brief and awkward answer. Other interests clamored for his attention. *Where is George? Is Sister Rachel okay? When did boys start noticing my little girl?* He suddenly realized *he* was nervous. He then realized that Barry was saying things that did interest him.

"George called earlier today. He and Sister Rachel have been delayed in Los Angeles because of an earthquake."

"Are you telling us that they are not here?" asked Anne. Not waiting for an answer, she probed, "Why were we not told? Why did you have us drive out here when she is not here?"

"Because George wants to show you something," answered Barry.

Though intrigued, Pastor Donovan and Anne remained stationary as the intern turned to escort them to the building. "Hold on just a minute," reacted Payne. "We're not sure about this. We came to see the sister, not whatever it is that George wants to show us."

"Trust me, you will want to see it."

The confidence that Barry exuded made Pastor Donovan wonder, *Is he going to show us the reliquary and cord? Or, better yet, is he going to show us his work in the lab and then give Joshua's ashes to Anne?* Although he processed the offer for less than a minute, he acquiesced. "We might as well see what it is, Anne. We are here. What can it hurt?" She gave no expression as they headed into SarkiSystems. He, however, looked as if each step supplied another answer to his "What can it hurt?" question.

Barry led them right through the initial meeting room, down the hallway, and into the boardroom. "Please, have a seat," directed Barry. "George is sorry that your plans for tonight did not work out the way you wanted. Nevertheless, he will be pleased to know that you stayed to hear the latest update on what is happening with our plans." He dimmed the lights in the room and announced, "The video you are about to watch is much longer than the first one you saw in this room. It goes into much more detail about the demand sector of the operation." With this said, he started the video and then left the room.

The video began with a dark screen. Only the voice of Lewis Barnone—the virtual anti-Christ begotten at SarkiSystems—was heard. "In the beginning, God created the heavens and the earth . . ." After reading the creation account, and emphasizing, "And God saw that it was good," the voice paused (with the screen still black), and then stated, "But every man did what was right in his own eyes. And this is the result." The screen suddenly became alive with graphic and horrific images of human suffering, starting with the widespread consequences of pandemics spread through international travel. Payne and Anne (father and daughter, pastor and pastor's kid) averted their eyes from the screen as Lewis Barnone narrated cadaverous footage (whether actual or not) of food shortages, air traffic and nuclear disasters.

"I can't believe we are a part of all this," whispered Anne. "Not the inheritance of humanity's sin, but of George's plan to right it all by bringing Jesus back."

"Anne, I'm sorry that I said 'yes' to Barry." He could see that she did not want to be there. "I was hoping that George wanted to show us the lab and that they were done examining Joshua's body and that he would give you an urn with the remains." As he whispered this to her, she got up and walked out of the room. Pastor Donovan did not know what to think, but he did think. *Did I upset her? Why did I mention Joshua and his remains? Maybe she just needs some fresh air. Maybe she just can't stand hearing how bad things are. Maybe she just needs to go to the restroom.* Unsure as to why she left, but confident that she would return soon, he decided to pay attention to what George wanted to show them. As he faced the screen, the audio and visual description of the current impact of power grid and water supply attacks intrigued him, as did the simulation of the coming impact of asteroids and falling space debris. The extensiveness of human depravity and cosmic vengeance, and thus the impending demise of planet Earth, captivated Pastor Donovan. Having become mesmerized by the projection, the video's abrupt, even unfinished ending startled him, as did the fact that Anne was still not back.

Before he had a chance to worry, before he spiraled down into a dark place crowded with suspicions, assumptions, and "what ifs," Anne entered the room with Barry by her side. She decreed, "It's time for us to go."

Thankful that she was all right, yet unsure that all was right, Pastor Donovan compliantly exited the room, exited the building, and exited the parking lot. All the while, he wondered, *Why was it time to go? Was it because the video concluded? Is she still upset about me mentioning Joshua? Did something happen to her while she was out of the room?* He wanted to be in the know, yet he remained silent. Was she dismayed? Relieved? Tired? Though curious, he could not get a good read on Anne. The only clue she offered occurred halfway home in the form of a terse announcement, "We'll talk about it tomorrow."

It? What exactly is the "it" that we will talk about? Again, for some reason, Pastor Donovan chose to be silent. Whether because of patience or avoidance, he chose to wait until tomorrow. And when they arrived home, the rest of the family had to choose to wait, too, for Anne went straight to her bedroom and closed the door.

* * * * *

Payne stood at the front door when he returned home the next day after a full day of pastoring at the church and at the hospital. Before entering the house, he decided to sit in one of the veranda chairs on the front porch to pray for the evening's powwow *and* to savor the aroma of Ashley's dinner creation.

"Smells delicious, Honey," hollered Payne as he plopped down on the living room couch. "What's for dinner?"

"That's a good question, Dad," said Doug as he made his way into the room from the hallway. "Mom told me not to bother her while she cooked. She closed the doors and has been in the kitchen ever since I got home from school."

"I smell bacon," said Payne with a smile.

"I do, too. But I also smell cookies. You don't think Mom would make bacon cookies, do you? I mean, most of her recent experiments have been bearable, but bacon-wrapped cookies? I don't think so."

"Dinner is ready," announced Ashley as she opened the door to the kitchen. "Someone please go tell Anne that we're ready."

The meal turned out not to be an experiment. Ashley simply fixed breakfast for dinner. The family devoured the bacon, eggs, and hash browns, leaving no leftovers.

"Mom, that was delicious," said Doug, "and not one of your new creations."

Payne quickly interceded when he saw puzzlement on Ashley's face. "Honey, what he's trying to say is that his 'superhero sniffer' detected (from the other room) the smell of bacon *and* some kind of cookies, maybe even bacon cookies."

"Bacon cookies?" Anne's quizzical inquiry triggered table laughter, a family custom missing for some time.

"You've always had an active imagination," said Ashley. "And, if you want to talk about food creations, then let's talk about how you put peanut butter on your hot dogs."

"Let's not," said Anne. "It's gross. Why anyone would do it is beyond me."

"Because *it* tastes good."

"As stimulating as this conversation is," interjected Payne, "peanut butter hot dogs and bacon cookies are not the 'it' that I came home to talk about. I want to hear from Anne about what happened last night. And I'd like to hear about it now, Anne, if that's okay with you."

Laughter ceased as Ashley cleared the table and as Anne cleared her throat. "The first thing I want to say is, 'Thank you, Dad, for not forcing me to talk about *it* last night. I know that not knowing was hard for you, but I needed time to digest what happened."

Payne eyed Doug, cutting off his son's "Just like I need extra time to digest peanut butter hot dogs" wisecrack. He also invited Ashley to sit down. Their dishes could wait, but not their attention.

"We did not see Sister Rachel last night. Instead, we saw a gory video about how awful the world is and why . . ."

"My friends saw something like that, too," interjected Doug. "Everyone is talking about it at school. It's all over the Internet."

"And that's exactly what George wants. He wants everyone to see how widespread evil is on this weary planet. He's constructing the need, fabricating the longing for Jesus' second coming."

"But you only saw the very beginning, Anne," said Payne.

"Yes, but I saw all that I needed to and more than I wanted to. That's why I left the room. Once outside the boardroom, however, I wanted to see more—not of the video, but of the lab that was right in front of me. This was my chance to see what they were doing with my baby."

"So while Dad watched a video on 'demand,'" surmised Doug, "you entered the 'supply' room."

"Well, not exactly. The door to the lab was locked."

"Did you knock?"

"No. I didn't have to. With my hand still on the knob, Barry opened the door. He looked bewildered with me standing right there before him. He asked me why I was not watching the video. I told him I wanted no part of what was happening in that room. Then I asked him if I could see the lab. He just stood there in his white coat. So, we stood there together, looking at each other, endeavoring to deduce what the other really wanted to say."

"So what happened?" asked Ashley in a manner that indicated that she was fully engaged.

"Barry told me that it was not a good time or idea for me to tour the lab. He then led me through a door to the outside where there were a few tables and benches. We sat alone, staring at each other."

"Sounds romantic," spouted Doug.

Payne noticed a slight blushing, but not nearly what she showed in the parking lot just twenty-four hours earlier. "Did you just sit there, or did you actually talk?"

"We talked."

"So while I listened to Lewis Barnone, you listened to Barry the intern?"

"Yes. But I did not just listen. I talked. He listened. We connected on a level that was both profound and vulnerable. We revealed classified information we may regret."

"So what did you talk about?" asked Ashley, now more engaged but less patient.

"After Barry explained why he took me out to where the workers eat— it's a place where there are no security cameras and therefore where we could talk freely—he divulged why Sister Rachel was not there."

"He told us why last night. He told us that she and George were delayed in Los Angeles because of an earthquake," recalled Payne while sporting an unimpressed look on his face.

"Yes, but Barry explained *why* they were in Los Angeles. Evidently George was concerned that Sister Rachel was not in favor of the plan. He took her to Las Vegas and Hollywood to show her that the world was in fact depraved. Because she had lived a sheltered life among the sisters, he took her on this trip to convince her that she was doing the right thing."

"So, let me get this straight," said Doug. "For my sister, his plan was to take her on a pilgrimage to the Holy Land. But for the sister, his plan was to take her on a pilgrimage to the twin Sin Cities, today's Sodom and Gomorrah?"

"That's right."

"No," roared Ashley. "None of this is right. That man should never have done what he did. He should never have taken the two of you anywhere. He has no right, no authority to do what he does."

"He also has no power," said Anne. "He may have created a seismic fearmonger in Lewis Barnone, but he could not keep the earth from quaking and cracking airport runways and his best laid plans. And this brings me to what I said to Barry. I shared with him the part I played in George's plan. I told him everything—the initial meeting, the implantation, the trip overseas, the kidnapping and suicide, meeting the sisters, the trip home, my baby's death and that I did not get to hold or see him. I told him everything. And I could see in his eyes that he was listening with his heart."

Payne marveled at how poised Anne recalled the conversation. At the same time, he did wonder, *Is there something she's not telling us? Some secret that will change everything? Did the intern slip up? Does she now hold the trump card? If so, how long will it be until she plays it and this whole thing can be over?*

"I asked him what he thought about Sister Rachel. He concurred with George that she seems unconvinced, merely going through the motions with a plan that she has yet to buy into, but is very much a part of. I intrigued Barry with my own assessment that she only agreed to come (or that the sisters only agreed to send her) here to rescue the blessed cord. I told him that her willingness to get pregnant shows just how far she was willing to go. She's only going along with the plan for the sake of the cord. She is George's Mary solely to be near the cord and in a position to return it to its rightful guardians."

"And what did the intern say to that?" asked Ashley.

"Not a whole lot, though he remained interested in all that I said."

"Did you talk about anything else?" asked Payne, probing for that hidden surprise.

"No. He looked at his watch and informed me that the video was about to end and that we must go." Anne paused, then disclosed to the family, "As he stood up, his identification tag, the one clipped to his coat, rested at eye level right in front of me. I could not *not* see it." Anne paused again, yet this time for more than a few heartbeats.

"So what did the badge say?" asked Ashley while exercising no patience.

"It said Barry B. Carlson."

The living room became deadly silent when Anne dropped the bombshell. Though he anticipated some kind of shocker, Payne did not see this seismic revelation coming. *He's the son of George? He's in on all this? How in the world are we going to free the sister now that he knows what we think?*

"I think we can trust him," stated Anne. "I saw it in his eyes. I thought about it all night and all day today. I believe he will help us."

"You may have thought about it all last night and today, but we didn't," asserted Ashley. "We will undoubtedly rehearse this nightmare all night and beyond, and we will have to do it without having seen his eyes." Ashley hesitated, as if contemplating whether or not she wanted to say something, nonetheless she continued, "But this is not the way I wanted to spend the evening. Tonight is the night before Valentine's Day and your father and I have our own Valentine's Day Eve tradition. It involves homemade strawberry-rhubarb pie and things that we do not need to go into; but let's just say that now I will not be in the mood to celebrate."

"So that's what I smelled," exclaimed Doug, eager to defend his superhero sense of smell and to dodge his mother's TMI exposé. "Not bacon cookies, but bacon and pie combined into one sweet aroma." Doug paused to smile, then asked, "Since you and Dad are not going to, well, you know, 'celebrate,' can I have a piece of pie before I go to bed? I mean, you worked so hard on it and your pies always taste so good, especially when they are so warm and fresh."

Payne watched Ashley get up to wash the dishes. He watched Doug get up to find a knife to cut the pie. He watched Anne let Bundt lick clean her plate under the table. He stayed seated at the table, thinking about what was just said. He could not believe that he missed the fact that Barry's last name was Carlson. He also could not believe that he missed the fact that tonight was Valentine's Day Eve. As he got up to go to bed (for it had been a long day), he smiled at the irony. *Why—especially on this night—does it have to be the pie, and not the wife, that is warm and fresh?* That was his last smile before he fell asleep.

* * * * *

"So what are we going to do?" Though voiced by the youngest Donovan, this question was *the* question on the mind of all four at the breakfast table.

"Doug, I think we need more time to think," said Payne on behalf of the family. "Because of what we now know, we all need to think about our thinking."

"So thinking is rethinking," surmised Doug.

"Sure, and you can't hurry rethinking."

"So what do we do while we rethink?" asked Ashley.

"I'm not sure," admitted Payne. "But I do know what we will *not* do. We will not force the issue or the hand of God. We—*I*—will not do anything until we all pray about it and talk about it."

"So we will 'stop, look, listen' before we proceed to rescue the sister." Doug's pithy yet mature comment reminded Payne that his children are a blessing, wise beyond their years. His son's remark also reminded him that people do at times remember his sermons, especially as Doug then parroted him verbatim: "We don't want to get blindsided as we step out into the traffic of ministry."

"I say we just ask George to release her," voiced Anne.

"You also say we should just trust his son," blurted her brother with more than a little disapproval. Evidently he forgot that he had previously suggested the very same idea.

"Okay," said Payne, before anything else could be said and while musing, *They are a blessing, though a blessing in progress.* Then he continued, "Stop. Look. Listen. That's our plan. We will think and pray, and wait upon the Lord to give us wisdom and strength to do what is right and good." The kids' immediate compliance and exit from the kitchen brought relief and suspicion. The quiet also made Payne aware that Ashley had been rather submissive during the morning exchange. *Is she on board with this? Was she up all night thinking about the Barry bombshell? Has she given up? Does she know that she is a blessing, a treasure that I am equally yoked with and committed to?* With only the two of them now in the room, and Ashley posturing herself to speak, he knew he was about to find out.

"Payne, I feel like you want to include us."

Ashley's cadence convinced him that a "however" was coming.

"I feel like you want to include me."

However.

"I know you trust me, that you value my input."

However?

"It's different now. We're together on a common mission."

So relieved that there was no "however," Payne affirmed, "We *are* a team using the same playbook." He then exclaimed, "The two shall become one!"

"Well," said Ashley with a tease in her voice, "I wouldn't say we've gone *that* far, at least not yet. How about you and I have some pie tonight?"

Payne liked her suggestion! He smiled as he got up to give her a kiss good-bye. He kept that smile warm and fresh as he got into the car. *This is turning out to be a very nice Valentine's Day.* This thought got blindsided, however, by another thought on the drive to church. *Someday the kids are going to have their own very nice Valentine's Days.* Though Payne could not wait for his tonight, he could wait for theirs. He knew that someday his "blessings" would find their own special blessings; he just was not in any hurry for the inevitable to happen. He knew Doug was in no hurry, but he was not so sure about Anne. As he approached the intersection where Ashley's accident had occurred, he wondered, *Has Anne been smitten by the intern? Is she ready for this? Does she not know how much this complicates things? Is this clouding her judgment? Can we trust Barry?* Though the questions piled up, Pastor Donovan remained unscathed through the intersection and all the way to the church and into his study where he could create space and time to "stop, look, listen," and to anticipate the celebration!

10

By focusing on recent developments and the quest to free the sister, Pastor Donovan had overlooked the wedding scheduled for Saturday. The couple wanted to get married on Valentine's Day, but a weekday service would have prohibited their out-of-town family and friends from attending. Thus, the couple reserved the church for the following Saturday, and they asked Pastor Donovan to officiate. Though he knew about this event well in advance, he found himself and his message unprepared. *What shall I say to the couple? What subject should I focus on?*

He decided to talk about the blessing of physical love in marriage—partly because he had a message about it on file, and partly because he had it on his mind. Standing before the bride and groom (two people eager to begin their just-hours-away honeymoon) and their family and friends, Pastor Donovan proclaimed this biblical yet neglected topic in the church. Using the Song of Solomon, an entire book of the Bible that celebrates human sexuality, he shared that physical love, at its best and by God's design, is mutual. After reading what amounts to the bride's wedding vow to her man in the sixteenth verse of the second chapter ("My beloved is mine, and I am his"), he explained to the couple that physical love is a combination of attraction and commitment, not a performance. Again quoting the bride, this time from the tenth verse of the seventh chapter ("I am my beloved's, and his desire is for me"), Pastor Donovan reminded the couple and all who were present that physical love is exclusive. "The bride did not say, 'I am my beloved's, and his desire is for his coworker or my best friend or anyone else.' She knew and the groom knew that their undivided love for each other would be one of the greatest gifts they would give to each other and to their children." He then proceeded to tell them that physical love is total, that they are marrying a person—not a body, a cook, or a security blanket, but a person to love wholeheartedly.

Because the couple's backs faced their family and friends, Pastor Donovan knew that he was the only one positioned to discern their hint of embarrassment. He also knew that this hint would soon become a clear and present blushing. "The final thing I want to say is that the physical love between a husband and wife is beautiful." He read from the fifth chapter of the Song of Solomon where the bride describes her groom, including where she likens his abdomen to carved ivory and his legs to pillars of alabaster. It wasn't, however, until Pastor Donovan read the first nine verses of the seventh chapter, the groom's description of his bride, that the couple could not hide their embarrassment, even to all the people behind them. Though they (the bride and groom, the family and friends, and, if truth be told, the preacher) were self-conscious, they all listened as the man in the Bible likened the curves of his wife's hips to jewels and her breasts to two fawns, twins of a gazelle. Only the sound of the pastor's voice (and maybe the groom's beating heart!) could be heard in the sanctuary as he concluded his message with verses he had memorized: "Your stature is like a palm tree, and your breasts are like its clusters. I said, 'I will climb the palm tree, I will take hold of its fruit stalks.' Oh, may your breasts be like clusters of the vine, and the fragrance of your breath like apples, and your mouth like the best wine!" Before turning the page in his little minister's book to the vows and rings portion of the ceremony, Pastor Donovan spontaneously pronounced a summary blessing on the couple, "May the Lord bless you with physical love that's mutual, exclusive, total, and beautiful—to His glory and your joy!"

After the wedding service and the reception, as the couple drove off to celebrate at an undisclosed location, Pastor Donovan sought refuge in his study. He needed his own time away from people. He also needed time to prepare for the next morning's sermon. For a moment, a very brief moment, he considered using the message he just gave and scrapping the one already printed in the bulletin. His tired self thought, *Since only a few at the wedding would be in attendance, why not?* He knew this was not a good reason, though he did smile at the thought of what Brother Bob might have said after the service. Still smiling, Pastor Donovan began to prepare the scheduled sermon, a message entitled "The Blessed Welcome."

* * * * *

Pastor Donovan stared at his scribbled notes as he stood behind the pulpit and delivered the message. "With the beatitudes, Jesus presents the blessed welcome. Here, at the beginning of the famous Sermon on the Mount, He let's all those listening to Him know that what He is about to say is for them, that the life He is about to describe is for them. Jesus hangs an 'Open' sign on the door to God's kingdom and let's His listeners know that they may enter into this life with God. Contrary to the Pharisees' politics of holiness, they, the ones in the crowd—the poor in spirit, those who mourn, and the rest—are not automatically written off or blackballed, but, in fact, are offered the blessed welcome."

Though Pastor Donovan knew that what he was saying was good news to his parishioners, he also knew that his interpretation was contrary to what they have heard and believed about the beatitudes. He especially knew this to be the case when he stated, "When Jesus said, 'Blessed are the poor in spirit,' He was not telling us to be poor in spirit. He is not giving a commandment here anymore than when He elsewhere says, 'Blessed are the poor.' If that were the case, then the majority of us here, if not all of us in this sanctuary would be unblessable. We do not meet the condition to be blessed. But, thank God, this is not what Jesus is saying. There is nothing inherently righteous about having nothing to give. To lack spiritual clout or formal training or means to do spiritual work like teach a Bible study or clothe the naked is not what makes us blessed. The poor in spirit are not blessed because they are poor in spirit. They are blessed because the kingdom of God is available to them. And, I might add, it's available also to the rich in spirit and the rich."

Pastor Donovan took a deep breath and, during what amounted to a dramatic pause, considered what he was about to say and how it might provoke his people even more than if he had listened to his tired self and reused the wedding message. "If Jesus guest-preached here today, He might very well announce a different set of beatitudes: 'Blessed are the fat, the ugly, the tattoo-laden. Blessed are the uneducated, the unemployed, the nonathletic. Blessed are the divorced, the unwed mothers, the imprisoned.'" Still staring at his notes, though well aware of the stir he just made, possibly the same stir his Lord made with the original beatitudes, Pastor Donovan clarified, "Please understand me, I am not advocating these conditions. They're not entrance requirements for church membership, qualities every one of us here should have or aspire to have. The fruit of the Spirit is *not* being fat and ugly, divorced and a single mom." Pastor Donovan refused to look up, fearful he would inadvertently look directly at a particular parishioner as he announced these new beatitudes.

Up to this point, the risk of being misunderstood, even offensive, remained high. But with the sermon concluding, and knowing he was too far in to hide or turn back, he resolved to make eye contact with his congregation. "What I am saying, however, is that these people—whom the culture or the media or the church regard and treat as the unblessed—can in reality be blessed. Again, not because of their condition, but because they can, right now, just as they are, enter into a life with God. They are not excluded. *You* are not excluded. *I* am not excluded. It's open enrollment time for the kingdom of God, and no one will be denied access because of pre-existing conditions! God knows we all have pre-existing conditions and yet He still invites us to join His all-inclusive community where He is its prime sustainer and most glorious inhabitant. The invitation is to align with what He is doing in this world and to live the eternal kind of life where His Spirit enables us to become more and more the kinds of people who live as He intends. This is good news. This is the blessed welcome."

After the service, as he stood at the door to shake hands, Pastor Donovan wondered what the reaction would be to his sermon. *Did I hit a homerun? Did I strike out? Did I get hit by the pitch?* The feedback surprised him, mainly because, other than the usual cordial comments, there was no feedback. Not one parishioner felt offended. Not one questioned his take on the beatitudes. Not one wished he had changed his message. Not one. That is, until the last one in line stood before him. Now there was one who wished he had changed his message. *He, the pastor,* was that one, for there with his right hand extended, stood George Carlson—the one exception, in Pastor Donovan's eyes, to the blessed welcome. The unwelcomed one came to church and was extended the invitation.

"I'm sorry I could not give you the blessed welcome last week," said George with a genial smile. "As Barry told you, Sister Rachel and I were delayed in Los Angeles due to the earthquake."

"Some things are just out of our control," responded Pastor Donovan. The irony of this passive-aggressive statement may have gone undetected by George, but not by Anne whose unannounced presence startled both men.

"Hello, Anne. I was just telling your father that I'm sorry you did not get a chance to visit Sister Rachel last week. But I'm glad you did get to watch our latest video, even though it awaits final editing."

Pastor Donovan perceived Anne to be conflicted. She looked determined to seize opportunity and yet unsure if this was the time or the place. As he thought, *This must be what I looked like in the pulpit earlier,* his daughter went ahead and voiced her belief knowing that it went contrary to George's beliefs. "You need to release Sister Rachel into our care. She will be better off living with us than being retained and confined at SarkiSystems."

"That will not happen," insisted George.

"But it should," said Pastor Donovan, informing the mastermind that Anne was not alone in her assessment.

"It doesn't matter whether it should or shouldn't," reacted George. "We have invested too much into her—too much time and money has been committed to the baby she carries. We will not back out now. All of our research and planning and reputation are at stake. We cannot and will not let her go."

"Then we will have to take her," said Anne with great calm and resolve.

For a moment, the three remained still, surmising the consequences of what just happened. George broke the silence. "I must go now. Sister Rachel and I need to get to the airport." Just before he turned to leave, he said, "I almost forgot. Anne, Barry wanted me to tell you that he enjoyed getting to know you last Monday. He said he learned a lot."

With his arm around Anne, Pastor Donovan watched George step into the car awaiting him. As it drove away, the Donovan car, parked in the lot, came into view. Hunkered down inside sat Ashley and Doug, as if endeavoring to avoid and escape that unwelcomed man. While closing the door to the church, Pastor Donovan thought, *May all of us, especially Sister Rachel, enjoy the blessed escape.*

* * * * *

"I can't believe you talked to that man," stated Ashley after rinsing the dishes.

This statement struck a cord with Payne, either because his wife said nothing during the entire Sunday afternoon meal or because he intentionally said a lot but nothing about that man. Payne pushed back, "And I can't believe you hid in the car." Having said this, he immediately recanted. "I'm so sorry, Honey. I should not have said that."

"Yes, you should," said Ashley. "I was hiding, and I pulled Doug into hiding with me. When I said that I can't believe you talked to that man, I was trying to convey my admiration that you (unlike me) would have the nerve, I mean, the courage and boldness to face and confront George."

"Thank you, but really it was Anne who stood up to George and gave him a piece of her mind."

"What did she say?"

"I said that the sister should come live with us and that SarkiSystems had no right keeping her against her will." That Anne answered the question startled both of her parents, for, unbeknownst to them, she eavesdropped from just outside the kitchen.

"Well, that's not all you said," divulged Payne, inviting Anne into the kitchen and into the conversation. "The last thing you said to George was that we will take Sister Rachel from him."

"Cool," interjected Doug as he followed in right behind his sister. "And how will we do it?" His question held anticipation, not doubt.

With all four Donovans back in the kitchen and eager to plan a rescue, Payne convened a family powwow. Though tired from the morning's affairs and ready for his Sunday afternoon nap, he understood that no rest would come until they dealt with the matter at hand.

"I say we storm the building and yank her out," offered Doug rather zealously.

"I was thinking of something a little more diplomatic," countered Payne with a smile, believing—or, at least, hoping—his son jested.

"Diplomacy will never work," contended Ashley. "That man will never concede. Anne was right, we will have to take her from him. But how?"

"Storm the building."

"Doug, we will not storm the building," insisted Payne, this time without a smile.

"If *we* won't, then who?"

"The police," said Ashley. "We'll go to the police."

"And what do we tell them?" Like Doug earlier, Payne asked with hope and anticipation, not doubt. "What do we report to them?"

The four paused for a collective gathering of thoughts. Breaking the silence, Doug announced, "I know," then hesitated before continuing. "This may sound weird, but Dad, your question reminded me of a dream I had last night." As Doug hesitated yet again, Payne wondered, *Is he formulating another joke? Or, is he trying to remember the dream? This better be good.* "In my dream I asked Sister Rachel's baby, 'Are you the expected one, or do we look for someone else?' The baby answered, 'Go and report what you see. SarkiSystems is involved in human cloning, fear mongering, and child abduction.' And just before I awoke, the baby said, 'Blessed is the one who keeps from stumbling over me.'"

"Human cloning *is* illegal," reasoned Payne.

"And so is kidnapping," said Ashley.

"Both are against the law," exclaimed Payne. "But we need proof. The police will want proof. So, how do we get it?"

"Barry," replied Anne. "He can provide the evidence."

"Can we really trust him?" asked Ashley.

"We can, and we must. He is the only one we know that can get us what we need. In my heart, Mom, I really do believe we can trust him."

"If, and I do mean *if* we can trust him, then how do we contact him?"

"Well," said Anne, as if searching for an answer to her mom's question, "George did say today that he and the sister were off to the airport, undoubtedly for the next leg on her pilgrimage."

"So, are you saying that, since George will be gone, we just go and ask Barry to help us? That he simply join with us in freeing Sister Rachel and in shutting down his father's operation?"

"Yes. Unless, of course, you have a better plan."

No one said a word, not even Doug.

"Okay then," uttered Payne, "I will call tomorrow and make an appointment to see Barry the intern."

"I'm going with you when you go," said Anne.

Payne assumed that would be case, just as he assumed Ashley would hunker down at home and have Doug keep her company.

11

WITH ANNE'S NOD OF approval (for she stood by his side listening in on the conversation), Payne said, "Anne and I will meet you this afternoon." *That was too easy*, thought Pastor Donovan as he hung up the phone. Not only did Barry answer his call, but the intern seemed intent, even anxious on meeting that day.

Barry greeted them when they pulled in to the parking lot. This time, instead of uneasiness surfacing because George was not the one standing there to welcome them, Pastor Donovan felt hopeful. Anne's composure fortified his confidence that what they were doing was right, that the one welcoming them can and must be trusted. Barry said very little as he ushered them around the building to the outside area where the tables and benches were and where the cameras were not.

"This whole plan that George conceived must be stopped," asserted Anne immediately as they sat down. "Human cloning is illegal and immoral. And so is kidnapping. Barry, I know you see it. Sister Rachel does not want to be here. She is being held against her will."

"Barry," interjected Pastor Donovan, "were you aware of what they were doing here at SarkiSystems?"

The intern glanced to his right and left, then leaned in toward them. "When I signed up for this internship, I thought I was going to be conducting research for Alzheimer's patients. I quickly found out that that was not the case. The advancements in disease therapies that I read about online turned out to be a front for their real work."

"So why did you stay?" asked Payne.

"I needed the internship," answered Barry, "plus the whole field of cloning is fascinating and promising."

"But it's wrong," insisted Anne.

"Only if it's *human* cloning," countered Barry.

"But *divine* cloning is okay? Is that what you are saying?"

"No, Anne, that is not what I am saying—not even close. What I am trying to say, Anne, is that stem cell research has brought many marvelous advancements in preventing and healing diseases. This is the wave of the future, and I don't want to miss it. I want to be a part of it."

"But not the illegal and immoral part of it," inserted Payne.

"Exactly. So I became increasingly troubled as I deciphered more and more what we were doing in the lab. And then when I met Anne, and especially when we talked right out here, I knew that I could not stay here."

"But you are still here."

"Yes I am, Anne, because, as I said, I need this internship. But I have a feeling I will not be here much longer. I'm fairly confident Mr. Carlson suspects that I am defecting. He was not too pleased when I raised questions about the infant we were working with. And Anne, when I realized it was yours, I took extra care with each step of the research."

"You mean as you sliced up my son and then cremated his little parts," said Anne with disdain.

"I am not proud of this," said Barry. "I truly am sorry, especially when I found out why we were doing what we were doing. Cloning flesh and blood may have merit with limitations, but endeavoring to clone a soul and spirit is arrogant and humanly impossible. Only God can send us His only begotten Son."

"We need your help," announced Pastor Donovan with urgency. The biblical reference increased his trust in the intern and in the plan to end all this coercive nonsense. "We need evidence to take to the police that George is involved in illegal human cloning."

"And that he is keeping Sister Rachel against her will," added Anne.

"But if you use evidence against Mr. Carlson, then why would you not use it against me?"

"I guess you will just have to trust us," said Anne. Barry's countenance change as she continued, "But not as much as we have to trust you since you are George's . . ."

"You must leave now," unleashed Barry.

Pastor Donovan could see that Barry's focus was not fixed on Anne's words but on the door to the building. "Is everything okay?"

"Please! Hurry! Go back to your car the way we came. Trust me. You must. Go now. I can't believe they're . . ."

The Cord

Pastor Donovan stood, not to run, but to focus. With his hand on Anne's shoulder, for she remained seated and still on task to recruit Barry, he watched the intern's demeanor turn from panic to surrender. He then saw the cause of this change. Out from the swung-opened door marched George. He appeared determined and irate.

"What are they doing here?" shouted George while maintaining a steady march. "I left you clear instructions not to let them on these premises." Nobody moved or said a word, either because of fear or because any action would be futile. "Barry, go pack your belongings. You are no longer an intern here at SarkiSystems."

Still standing and still focused, Pastor Donovan observed subtle indicators that Barry was conflicted, that he was both devastated and relieved. But there was something else, something deeper that Payne could not quite read as he watched the intern make his final entrance into the building. *He looks convinced, but what about?*

"Look here," said George, directing their attention to him and off the fired intern. "After what you said yesterday, you are not welcomed here. You are not to be near Sister Rachel. How can I trust you after you said that you will take her from me?"

"You can't," retorted Anne. "You can't trust us and we can't trust you."

"What happened?" asked George, still riled at their presence at SarkiSystems.

"We came to our senses," answered Pastor Donovan. Even though he could see that George was averse to any response, he continued, "What happened was we saw that your supply and demand was manmade. It's artificial; an imitation of what in fact is real. And what in fact is real will be supplied and demanded by God in His timing and in His way. And we cannot force Him to do otherwise, no matter how much we plan or how hard we try."

"You're asking *us* what happened?" Anne stood as she addressed George. "We should be asking *you* what happened! What made you think that you could do what only God could do, that you could compel and guarantee the divine prerogative? What happened, George? What got into you? Pride? Curiosity? Presumption? Ambition? Power? Fear? Greed? Anger? What happened? Did 'Legion' rise up from the sea and enter you?"

Anne's fury dissipated when the door to SarkiSystems opened. All conversation ceased as Barry approached his former employer and the father-daughter team. Pastor Donovan could see that the intern carried something in his hand, but he could not discern the object. The tension at hand caused his thoughts to run wild. *Is that a gun? Has he gone mad? Is he so disgruntled that he is going to kill George? Is he going to kill us? Is he going to commit a fifteen-minutes-of-fame murder-suicide?* Payne's fear, like Anne's fury, dissipated as Barry advanced and as the object became discernably not a weapon.

"Before I go," stated Barry, "I want to give Anne the ashes we promised her." Pastor Donovan could not believe that he thought the beautifully crafted box that Barry handed to Anne was a gun. He also could not believe how boldly the intern acted in front of George and how tenderly he spoke to Anne. "When I found out that you were the mother of the baby being studied, I began to make this wood urn. I modeled it after the reliquary because these remains deserve our respect, too. They contain the proof that the plan continues and that hope remains."

"Hope remains," echoed Anne with intrigue. "They are 'hope remains'—Joshua's remains contain our hope. Don't they?"

Pastor Donovan observed the two reading each other's eyes, desperately discerning whether they now shared a common distrust, anger, or conspiracy. All eyes, however, immediately refocused on the urn as George seized it from Anne's hands and lifted its cover. His eyes investigated the contents while his hands scrutinized the fashioned wood. With a dismayed look, as if he expected to find further incriminating evidence against his sinister defector, he closed the cover and then, while he handed the urn back to Anne, he asserted, "You and your father are to leave now. You are no longer welcomed here. And Barry, you are to go collect your things, as I already instructed you to do, and then leave, never to return."

The four walked through the door that moments before George flung open. Barry turned to go into the lab to gather his belongings. Pastor Donovan and Anne made their way down the hallway as George stood watch by the sister's bedroom door, protecting his investment and ensuring that everybody did as he or she was told.

Not wanting to see again the boardroom or the photos on the walls, Payne stared straight ahead. Even when Anne shouted "Soon" as they passed George and the closed bedroom door, he stayed focused on the door in front of them—the one that would lead them into the room that he first entered to begin it all but would now lead them out to their car and into the plan to end it all. As he watched Anne carefully sit in the passenger seat and cradle the urn, he thought, *What is our plan now? What did this visit accomplish? Should we have even come?* Before too many questions piled up, and before exiting the parking lot, he perceived that Anne, though riding shotgun, sat in the driver's seat. He could see that she had a plan.

"Dad, we need to go home right away," muttered Anne like a ventriloquist. Though he heeded what she said, how she said it perplexed him. *Does she sense someone might be reading her lips? Is she speaking for the object in her hands?* No matter the reason, he continued to listen as they drove out the parking lot and straight home. "This box—Joshua's ashes—contains the proof we need. I don't know how, but Barry gave us the evidence we need to take to the police."

"How do you know this?"

"I could see it in his eyes," answered Anne with full expression now that they were heading home and away from surveillance. Pastor Donovan marveled at her confidence and at the way she cuddled the handcrafted box the whole way home.

"What is Doug doing out in the street?" asked Payne as they turned onto their block.

"He's telling us to hurry," discerned Anne.

While careful not to hit his son, Payne pulled up right beside him in haste. Anne rolled down her window so they could hear Doug's frantic news. "Barry called and said that George found out about the thumb drive and that he's getting ready to leave with the sister."

"Barry's taking Sister Rachel?" asked Payne with a puzzled voice and look.

"No, Dad. George is, and he's taking her far away. He's packing their bags right now. Barry said that he's very upset."

"Barry's upset?"

"No, Dad. George is upset—something about finding out that Barry had downloaded unauthorized information. He became suspicious when he entered the lab to reprimand and remove Barry and saw experiments still being done. Somehow George knew that the time was not yet right to give the ashes to Anne—something about he would do so when the research was fully completed. So Barry said George went straight to the computer, clicked a few keys, and determined that files had been downloaded."

"Doug, what's this about a thumb drive?" probed Anne.

"Barry placed a thumb drive with downloaded files in the ashes."

"So Barry buried it?"

"Yes, Dad. And he said it contains all we need; and that we need to take it to the police right away for there's no time to lose."

"What does mom think about this?" asked Payne. "Is she okay?"

"She doesn't know anything about all this. She's at the supermarket shopping for this week's meals."

"Then hop in the car."

Before reaching the end of the block, Anne insisted, "Dad, pull over." Though set on wasting no time, Payne yielded. He then watched and waited as Anne carefully handed Doug the urn like a mother would her newborn baby. "Doug, would you please reach in and dig out the thumb drive? I just can't touch Joshua's remains."

"So you want Doug to dig!" Payne could see that she did not appreciate his witty attempt to relieve tension.

"I got it," exclaimed Doug.

As the thumb drive appeared from the box like a phoenix rising from the ashes, Anne reasserted, "I knew it. I knew when he handed me the box that he was handing us what we needed. I just didn't know how, but now I know. Hope remains! I knew we could trust him. Let's go!"

In an attempt to make up time, Payne ignored the stop sign in front of him. In his rearview mirror, however, flashed lights that he could not ignore. Forced to pull over, he sat impatiently, staring at the approaching policeman through his side mirror. Not until the officer stood beside him and addressed him did he recognize that it was Officer Bedford.

"Hello, Officer. I'm Pastor Donovan. Last year you assisted my wife when she was in a car accident. I know I ran the stop sign, but you have to believe me, we're on our way to the police station. We have evidence of a man involved in human cloning."

"Slow down, sir," said the officer.

"I will, Officer," replied Pastor Donovan as he reached for the ignition. "I promise."

"Let me see your hands," asserted Officer Bedford. "And slowly step out of the car, sir."

"We don't have time for this," insisted Payne as he complied. "As we speak, he is leaving and taking her with him." Even with his hands against the car and being frisked, he continued, "Please believe me, human cloning is happening at SarkiSystems and the mastermind, George Carlson, has impregnated the sister and is taking her far away against her will. I know this makes no sense, but you have to believe me. We found the evidence—a thumb drive—in an urn."

"Officer, I can explain," said Anne as she leaned over toward the driver's window.

Apparently satisfied that they were not a danger or flight risk, Officer Bedford instructed the Donovans to step onto the sidewalk. With Anne now holding the box and Doug clapping ashes off his hands, Pastor Donovan presented the thumb drive. But before her dad could frenziedly expound some more, Anne spoke, "Officer, what my dad is handing you is the evidence we were taking to the police station. It contains proof of illegal cloning happening at SarkiSystems. But more importantly, and why we are in such a hurry, is that the one behind all this is right now kidnapping a girl that he forced his plan upon. We need to rescue her. Please trust us. Please help us!"

"If you don't trust us, then at least trust the evidence," said Doug. "Don't you have a computer in your police car? Plug in the drive and look at the files yourself."

There on the sidewalk that he often took walks on hand-in-hand with his kids, Pastor Donovan now stood amazed at their maturity and insights. He also stood ashamed at his inability to communicate. *They're now holding my hand*, he thought as Officer Bedford considered Doug's proposal.

"I can't do that," said Officer Bedford while examining the thumb drive, "but I can do this." Payne and the kids listened as he radioed the station about a possible 207 in progress at SarkiSystems. After he requested back up, Officer Bedford instructed the Donovans to return to their vehicle, follow the rules of the road, and meet him at SarkiSystems.

A thankful heart beat in Pastor Donovan as the police car raced away with lights flashing, mainly because hope did remain that Sister Rachel would soon be free, but also because Officer Bedford did not issue him a ticket. The ride to SarkiSystems proved to be taxing. Following the rules of the road when you're in a hurry can drain your patience and the patience of your passengers. "How many more stop lights, Dad?" "Can't you go any faster, Dad?" "How much further, Dad?" Payne seriously considered resurrecting the old parenting trick of suggesting, "Kids, let's play the silent game." Instead, however, he suggested that they use their energy to look out for George and to pray.

Ignoring the painted lines in SarkiSystem's parking lot, Pastor Donovan headed straight toward Officer Bedford and Barry. Anne panicked, "Is he arresting Barry?"

"Let's hope not," replied Payne as he parked beside the police car.

Far from finding the former intern in handcuffs and under arrest, the Donovans heard Officer Bedford asking systematic questions and Barry giving succinct answers. "And what color is the car?" "Charcoal grey." "How long ago did they leave?" "About ten minutes ago." "Which way did they go?" "They turned left out of the parking lot." "Where are they going?" "I have no idea." During this exchange, two back up patrol cars arrived.

"Please think, is there anywhere he might take her to? A house? A hotel? A hiding place? Somewhere he might think they cannot be traced?"

"Traced!" exclaimed Barry. "That's it. We can trace their exact location using the chip implanted in the sister." Pastor Donovan observed the wide-eyed looks on all the officers' faces while he thought, *Of course! George would have done to Sister Rachel what he did to Anne.* Barry explained, "I'll go get the laptop from the lab and bring it out here. We'll track their whereabouts, and Officer Bedford can relay the information to the rest of you officers by using the radio in his car."

Barry made his move to the building before Officer Bedford made an official decision. While the former intern disappeared into the building and the officers deliberated the aptness of an implanted chip, Pastor Donovan wondered, *What is Barry really doing right now? Is he going back into the lab to hide incriminating evidence? Is he going to lead the officers on a wild goose chase so George can get away? Can we really trust him?*

His questions would soon be answered because, with laptop in hand, Barry rushed out to the group. With bated breath they watched Barry punch computer keys. After catching his breath, Barry announced, "They are heading north on Biafield Road."

"Go," ordered Officer Bedford as he signaled the other officers. Pastor Donovan held on to Anne and Doug as the two police cars raced out of the parking lot. The three Donovans listened intently as Barry apprised Officer Bedford of George's location and as Officer Bedford radioed the officers in pursuit.

"It sounds like the back up doesn't need back up," remarked Doug as the gap narrowed between George and the police.

"It looks like they are heading toward the airport," announced Barry.

"Can't you alert the airport police?" asked Pastor Donovan. He could see that Barry's revelation troubled Officer Bedford.

"They will place the entire airport on lockdown," explained Officer Bedford. "We must apprehend him *before* he reaches the airport."

"If only we could scramble a few military drones or Apache helicopters," wished Doug.

"Helicopter. That's it!" boomed Officer Bedford.

"An Apache will capture George?" asked Doug with animation.

"No. But we have a helicopter making practice water drops out near the airport. With Barry giving us the exact location, the pilot might be able to slow down or divert the suspect away from the airport."

Pastor Donovan and Doug stood right by the police car, thoroughly engaged in the unfolding drama. Anne leaned against the family car, gently rocking the wood urn. With the two police cars still in pursuit and the police helicopter now dispatched, hope did not only remain; its fruition remained imminent. Father and son listened to every word broadcasted from and to the makeshift command post in the parking lot. Almost giddily, they bounced up and down as the action unfolded and they heard that the pilot was going to drop a load of water at the exit of an underpass that George was approaching. "This will get his attention," remarked the pilot over the radio as he released three hundred gallons of water. Though only seconds elapsed since the water entered the underpass on the one end and the car entered on the other, the radio silence during this time pierced Pastor Donovan. *What just happened? Did the plan work? Is that really George's car, or did some random citizen just get drenched?*

"The vehicle has not exited the underpass," reported the pilot. "It must have stalled when hit with the wave of water, or else hydroplaned into the side of the retaining wall."

"Dad, Sister Rachel is in that car," reminded Doug with a concern that now replaced the excitement of the chase. "Is she okay? Is the baby okay?" They both looked at Officer Bedford for answers.

"The officers are arriving now to the scene," stated Officer Bedford with an official sounding voice. "They will secure the area and give us a report."

The wait was not a few seconds, but a few excruciating minutes. Payne fought to keep hope afloat. Instead of drowning in regret and guilt for *all* that has happened, he chose to pray a blessing on the officers that were helping and on those that they were helping, those being the sister and the baby. He was not yet able to bless the driver.

"Air bags were deployed," radioed an officer. "The driver is conscious, but is experiencing stomach and back pain."

Serves him right, thought Pastor Donovan, taking a bit of pleasure in hearing God's vengeance.

"There are no other passengers," reported the officer on scene.

A collective "What?" bellowed out of father and son while sharing astonished looks with the officer and ex-intern.

"Repeat and confirm," radioed Officer Bedford.

"The lone passenger, the driver, is conscious, but is experiencing stomach and back pain."

"What did he do with her?" asked Pastor Donovan with utter disbelief. "Where is Sister Rachel? He wouldn't dump her on the side of the road, would he?"

"She will be airlifted to the hospital once the water bag is detached," announced the officer on scene.

"She?" came forth from all at the command center.

"Repeat and confirm," radioed Officer Bedford.

"The driver, who has no license but identifies herself as Sister Rachel, is being airlifted to the hospital once the water bag in detached from the helicopter."

"Where is George?" asked Doug with disbelief and curiosity. "What did she do with him? Did *she* dump *him* on the side of the road?"

Though very much interested in George's whereabouts, the mention of "water bag" caused Pastor Donovan's attention to remain on the one who is with child and experiencing stomach pains. He sought reassurance as he asked the officer, "Is the sister okay? Is the baby okay?"

Officer Bedford repeated what the officer on the scene officially reported. He reassured Pastor Donovan that the girl was safe and free for the moment, but that she will be questioned as to what happened. He then said, "She is on her way to the hospital where she will want to see her pastor. Go in peace, and obey the rules."

As the Donovans left SarkiSystems, Payne could see in his rearview mirror Officer Bedford holding out handcuffs and talking to Barry.

12

"STAY WITH YOUR MOM and let her know where we're going and why we're going," said Payne as he dropped off Doug at the house. He knew Doug would rather go to the hospital and continue the pursuit for hope and answers, but he also knew Ashley would be worried if she returned from the market to an empty house.

Pastor Donovan had driven to the hospital many times, but this visit felt different—a mortal host of fear, dismay, confusion, suspicion, and hope bombarded his pastor's heart and father's love. "Sister Rachel will sure be glad to see you," said Payne, projecting his own relief to have Anne by his side.

The hospital volunteer had no record of a Sister Rachel being admitted.

"That's impossible," explained Pastor Donovan. "A police helicopter transported her here less than a hour ago. She must be here."

"Please wait while I try to find her," said the volunteer. While still on the phone, she asked Pastor Donovan, "And who is wanting to see her?"

"I am her pastor," said Payne, playing the pastor card that permits him to see any patient at any time, even before and after visiting hours.

"And I'm her sister," said Anne, playing the family card, even though bluffing.

After the volunteer relayed their information and listened to the person on the other end of the line with undoubtedly more seniority, she wrote a room number on two visitor wrist bands and fastened them to the "pastor" and "sister."

"I can't believe she's here and not you know where," whispered Anne in the elevator, conscious of the camera mounted above them.

Amen, thought Pastor Donovan, *but where is you know who?* He instinctively reached for Anne's hand when the door opened. "I can't tell you how much this means to Sister Rachel that you are here." They double-checked the number written on their bands and together walked into the room. There before them on the bed wept a scared and weary young girl. Rocking back and forth and holding her stomach but not her tears, Sister Rachel sobbed repeatedly, "My baby. My baby. My baby."

Pastor Donovan grabbed a chair while Anne sat on the bed as an empathetic advocate and presence of hope. With her arms wrapped around the sister and with no need to whisper or pass secret notes in a replicated bedroom, Anne presented hope. "You are free, Sister Rachel. You are free!"

Pastor Donovan sat by the bed and watched the sister's countenance progressively change as the blessed truth penetrated her mind and diffused a ray of hope in her heart. He also watched the bond between the two girls strengthen as George's chains fell off. *She really is free*, he thought. *They are free. We are free. But what about George, is he free?* Though curiosity weighted him down, Pastor Donovan knew he needed to be patient. This was not the time to ask, "What happened? How did you escape? Where is George?" This was the time to ask, "Are you okay? How are you feeling? Where is the doctor?"

Some of his questions were about to be answered, for, as Anne wiped tears from the sister's cheeks, a doctor walked into the room. "I'm going to have to ask you to step out of the room as I examine the patient," said the doctor.

"Can she stay?" asked Sister Rachel, pointing to Anne.

"What relation is she to you?"

"I am her sister," said Anne abruptly.

"Is this true?" asked the doctor while looking directly at his patient. With her affirmative nod and smile, Pastor Donovan left the room alone with bifurcated sentiments. He felt thankful and relieved that the two were bonding and that Anne could be present to support. But he also felt somewhat unnerved that the two could so easily lie. Waiting outside the hospital room triggered a flashback of waiting outside the "bedroom" in the hallway at SarkiSystems. But instead of facing a framed photo of the reliquary, the wall in front of him showcased a painted mural of a rainbow festooned with storks carrying blue and pink bags. Only then did it dawn on him that Sister Rachel was admitted to the maternity ward. *Do they think she is in labor? Did her water bag break when the pilot's water bag broke and the car's airbag deployed? Can the baby survive such a premature birth? How come I don't hear any crying?*

"Are you okay?" asked a nurse.

"I have to know, is the girl in this room having her baby?"

"Sir, the girl in this room is not having a baby," said the nurse with a puzzled look.

Exhausted and unable to fathom any more surprises, Pastor Donovan slid down to the floor with his back against the wall. With a downcast, not pastoral voice, he muttered, "What do you mean she is not having a baby?"

"She's on this floor because there are no other open beds."

"Dad, you can come in now; the doctor wants to talk to you," announced Anne from inside the room.

"Doesn't sound like your daughter's having a baby," said the nurse as she helped Pastor Donovan off the floor, "at least not today. But before you know it, sir, that day will come. They grow up so fast." He donned a reticent smile, then, reaching out to whatever he could find for balance, he walked into the room.

"Please have a seat," said the doctor.

Is the news that bad? Or am I that bad? thought Pastor Donovan as he sat down.

"The car accident caused some trauma. She sustained a few bruises and a minor cut on her hand, and she is experiencing mild pain in her back. None of this concerns me. However, her abdominal pain, because she is pregnant, does concern me. But after examining her, I find nothing out of the ordinary. Everything seems to be normal regarding the baby."

If he only knew, thought Pastor Donovan, *just how wrong he was, that in fact everything is out of the ordinary and nothing is normal regarding the baby.*

"Because of this," declared the doctor, "I see no reason why she cannot go home." He looked at Sister Rachel and said, "So, unless you object, you are free to go. Just wait here a moment while I go sign the release papers."

The three said not a word as the doctor left the room, as if fulfilling a collective agreement not to jeopardize the release. Before they could grasp the weight of the imminent freedom, the doctor came in with the signed papers and the nurse that would escort them to the front of the hospital. As they exited the room, the doctor said to Pastor Donovan, "Just as a precaution, make sure she sees her obstetrician this week."

While the "sisters" held hands entering the elevator, Pastor Donovan held an interview with himself. *Does she have an obstetrician? Not anymore. We'll need to find one for her. The doctor said she can go home; so, where is home? I assume I'm taking her to our house. How long will she be staying? I have no idea.* When the elevator door opened, Officer Bedford stood before them, blocking the way to the front doors and to freedom.

"Where are you going?" asked the officer.

"She is going home," said the nurse. "The doctor just released her."

"And where is home?"

"She is staying with us," answered Pastor Donovan.

"Is everything okay, officer?" inquired the nurse, as if eager to fulfill her duty and return to her floor.

"I'll take her from here," said Officer Bedford. "You are free to go—you, nurse, not the sister."

With the nurse back in the elevator, Officer Bedford looked directly at Sister Rachel and said, "We have to talk."

"Can't it wait?" responded Anne while still holding the sister's hand. "She has been through a lot."

"That's what we must talk about," replied Officer Bedford, "and, no, it can't wait. She needs to come down to the station and answer questions about what exactly happened today."

"If it can't wait, can it at least take place at our house?" requested Pastor Donovan.

"I suppose that can be arranged," offered the officer, "but I will need authorization. We normally get both sides of the story as soon as possible and have both people available for further questioning."

"Both people?" inquired Pastor Donovan. He immediately envisioned Barry in handcuffs and forcing an ugly "he said, she said" interrogation. *I knew we could not trust him,* he thought while interpreting the concerned looks on the girls' faces.

"Yes, we have George Carlson down at the station. He is being held for questioning."

"George? You have George in custody?" Desperately trying to comprehend the last few hours (if not the last year), Pastor Donovan rattled off random questions. "Where did you find him? How did you find him? What was on the thumb drive? Do you have enough evidence? Do you have the cord? How did Sister . . ."

"Sir, there are many unanswered questions," interjected Officer Bedford, "and we intend to get answers for each and every one of them." With the girls physically shaking at the prospect of being in the same building with that man, Officer Bedford escorted them to seats in the lobby and then radioed for clearance to escort them to the Donovan's house.

Even with an impending police investigation, Sister Rachel's first steps outside the hospital resembled a child's first steps. For the first time since her flight to the new land, she could taste freedom. Like a proud daddy, Pastor Donovan cherished the moment but also housed concern for her safety. He drove carefully the whole way home, checking often his rearview mirror to make sure he did not upset Officer Bedford and, more notably, to watch his two girls in the back seat. *I am blessed and in need of a blessing*, thought Pastor Donovan as he observed Anne holding Sister Rachel's hand in one hand and Joshua's urn in the other *and* as he gripped the steering wheel with his left hand and rested his right hand on the empty seat beside him, a seat that reminded him that there stood one at home who would need space and time, both her own and his. *Lord, have mercy!*

* * * * *

"Why is he here?" asked Ashley from the front porch and pointing to the police car parked in front of the house.

"Honey, look who is here," said Payne rather bamboozled as he motioned to Sister Rachel walking right toward her. "And look who is not here. She is free, Honey."

"If she is free," countered Ashley, "then why is he here?"

"He is here to help," said Payne as the officer stepped out of the car. "Honey, do you remember Officer Bedford? He is the one who helped you when you had the accident. And he is here now to help Sister Rachel and to ask her about today's events and what led up to them." Payne held his wife as the officer greeted her and walked into the house.

Everyone congregated in the living room. Officer Bedford sat in the leather chair. Doug sat on the floor. Husband and wife sat on one couch. The inseparable sisters sat on the smaller couch. The urn sat on the mantel above the fireplace. Bundt paced in the backyard, banned from the gathering because of his neurotic behavior toward any uniformed invader of his territory.

"Before we officially begin, I want to ask, how are you doing since the accident?" Payne noticed Ashley sit up, as if to answer Officer Bedford's question, even though he directed it to Sister Rachel. Payne wondered, *Does she even know about the sister's accident? The water drop? The stomach pains? The wood box on the mantel? How much did Doug tell her?*

"I feel okay," said Sister Rachel, looking a bit overwhelmed and guarded.

"I'm glad to hear that," said Officer Bedford. "With all the bad news in the world today, it's nice to hear good news and to know that you and the baby are well."

Payne discerned an immediate climate of suspicion in the room triggered by the officer's concern. Maybe because of his tone, or maybe because of his cognizance of the "supply and demand," but Officer Bedford, no matter his true intentions, instantly lost the trust of those sitting in the living room. Payne marveled at how together they readied themselves, like a team in a no-huddle offence.

"Will this take long?" asked Ashley. "This girl obviously has been through a lot and needs time to rest."

"She has been through a lot," replied Officer Bedford with a tinge of realization that he's outnumbered and unwanted. "And that's why I'm here—to find out what she has been through. As soon as I get her statement about what happened, I will leave and she will be free to rest."

"Can I let Bundt in?" asked Doug with a sly smirk.

"Not yet," said Payne while concealing a menacing laughter, "but maybe later." Maintaining composure and a curiosity, he directed Sister Rachel, "Please tell the officer what happened today."

A brief but deep silence filled the room. Anticipation swallowed up all sound for a moment—no one talking, no clock ticking, no dog barking, no plane flying. Then, the sister spoke, not Sister Rachel, but Anne, her new sister-in-cord.

"I will tell you exactly what happened. When George found out that Barry downloaded incriminating evidence and passed it on to us, he knew that he had very little time to escape and to protect his investment. As he scurried to pack the essentials, I'm sure our resolve to take her from him echoed in his mind. At some point, while so focused, he became distracted. With his guard down, Sister Rachel seized an opportunity to grab his keys, push him into a room and lock it, and drive off in search of freedom. Unaware that police were pursuing her, she followed the flight of planes coming in for a landing." Anne looked right at Officer Bedford and said, "And, of course, you know what happened from there."

"Is that what really happened?" asked Officer Bedford.

"Yes," replied Sister Rachel, looking both surprised and impressed at Anne's depiction.

"Did Barry help you?" asked Anne.

"No."

"Then how did he know where you trapped George?" questioned Officer Bedford.

"I don't know."

He pressed, "How did Barry know that George was locked inside the room adjacent to the lab? How did he lead me straight to him as these folks drove off to meet you at the hospital?"

"Officer, I do not know."

"Now can I let him in?" mouthed Doug to his dad.

"Soon," whispered Payne with a smile. Turning to Officer Bedford, with a straight face and a hope to end the questioning, he summarized the day and the reason for the escape and rescue and the need for rest. "George Carlson, whom you have right now down at the station, lured this young girl into his elaborate scheme of human cloning. For nearly four months she has been held against her will. Today, she courageously found freedom. But her liberty came with a price. She suffered great pain because of her accident and ensuing concern for her baby." He paused, then with his pastor's voice, he said, "She's been through a lot, more than we can imagine, wouldn't you agree?"

Officer Bedford offered a reluctant nod of approval. Along with the others in the room, Pastor Donovan remained still and hopeful as the officer closed his notebook, informed Sister Rachel that she would need to be available for further questioning, and headed out to his patrol car. Once he heard the car door close, Payne suggested, "Doug, why don't you let Bundt in? I bet he wants to say good-bye to the officer!"

"And say hello to Sister Rachel," added Anne.

* * * * *

"I need to get the cord," avowed Sister Rachel as she sat on the couch and stared at the urn above the fireplace.

She may be free from George, but her hope remains attached to the cord, discerned Payne while Bundt and he stood watch at the front window to make sure the peace officer left them in peace.

"You must be hungry," said Ashley. "I'll go make something, something simple."

"Maybe bacon-wrapped cookies," shouted Doug from the kitchen, evidently making a snack for himself.

"You'll get used to him," said Anne as she sat facing Sister Rachel and holding her hand. "As for my mom's cooking, . . ."

"You'll get used to it, too," said Doug while entering the living room with a hotdog garnished with peanut butter.

"Actually, she's a great cook."

"World famous," muttered Doug with a mouth full of food.

Payne observed Sister Rachel during this banter. She looked as if she wanted to smile, but she refrained. *There's more to do*, thought Pastor Donovan as he walked away from the window. "Sister Rachel, do you know where the cord is?"

"It is back at SarkiSystems, in the room that I locked Mr. Carlson in."

"Unless the police took it as evidence," surmised Payne. "Barry may have given it to Officer Bedford or taken it for himself."

"He would not have done that," insisted the sister. "I trust him."

"I trust him, too," said Anne. "But I'm not so sure about Officer Bedford."

"I agree," said Doug. "How convenient that he just happened to be at the corner when he stopped us on the way to the police station—as if someone tipped him off, as if he and his informant were determined to stop that thumb drive from making it to the station."

"And did you hear him link the baby to the world news being thrust upon everyone?" added Payne, offering another piece of distrust. "Why would he do that unless he believes the baby supplies what the news demands?"

To everyone's surprise, including Bundt's, the doorbell rang. Immediately Payne looked out the window to see if the police car had returned. *Is he already back to ask further questions? Is he going to arrest the sister? Is he going to arrest all of us coconspirators?* Before his thoughts completely collapsed his world, he spotted Barry, not Officer Bedford, standing at the front door. "It's Barry," announced Payne. "Do I let him in?"

The sisters reacted with a resounding "Yes."

"I can't believe you are here," exclaimed Sister Rachel as Barry entered the house. "Are you okay?"

"I'm fine," said Barry. "But more importantly, are you okay?"

"I'm okay."

"What happened, Barry?" asked Pastor Donovan as if interrogating a suspect. "The last time I saw you the officer had his handcuffs out and facing you."

"Hearing that Mr. Carlson was not in the car made me remember that I saw the door to the cord's containment unit locked when I went in to get the laptop. At the time I thought it a bit odd that Mr. Carlson would have taken the time to close it and lock it since he would have had the cord and been in a hurry to leave. But, while standing outside with the officer, I deduced that the sister must have cunningly taken his keys, locked him inside the unit, and taken his car."

"So how did you know that she would be *here*?" asked Payne with a readiness to fuel his cynicism.

"I didn't, but after I left the police station, I ventured here in hopes of finding the sister."

"Why did you go to the station? And why did you not just ask the police where she was?" probed Payne.

"I went to the station to give my statement. They wanted my account of what happened. I did not ask about Sister Rachel's whereabouts because I did not want to risk Mr. Carlson overhearing."

"Thank you," said the sister.

"For what?" asked Barry.

"For taking care of me at SarkiSystems."

The one she trusted smiled, then revealed, "The officer who detained Mr. Carlson insisted on taking the cord. He said it was for evidence."

"So the blessed cord is at the police station?"

"Not exactly," said Barry. Taking a few steps closer to the couch and lowering his voice, he divulged, "I did give the officer the cord, the cord from your baby." He said this while looking directly at Anne. "George insisted on saving the cord in case something happened to *the* cord. He maintained that, in spite of it being one generation removed, the cord could still produce our coming King. Even though the descent would empty Him of the full appearance and likeness, it would preserve enough form to not void His return."

"That man is absolutely crazy," declared Anne.

"But absolutely committed," stated Barry.

"That man should absolutely be committed because he is absolutely crazy," construed Doug.

A collective "amen" came from everyone except Sister Rachel. She gazed upon Barry, as if he were a God-sent angel to bring good news. "Where is the blessed cord?"

"It is safe," announced Barry. "And now that I know you are here and safe, I will bring it to you."

A heavy burden has been lifted, an impossible mission has been accomplished, thought Payne as he observed freedom radiate from the sister. He then thought, *Maybe he can be trusted*, as he watched Barry walk out to his car.

"There is one for each of you, but I can make more," announced Ashley as she entered the living room with a plate of egg salad sandwiches. "Where's Barry? I made one for him, too."

"He just went out to his car," replied Payne with hesitancy. "But I'm not exactly sure why."

"I think he went to get the cord," conjectured Doug.

From the front window, Payne could see Barry closing the trunk to his car. He could also see Barry approaching the house and carrying something in his hands—something that he now knew was not a gun! Almost speechless, but able to time his words between breaths, he uttered, "He's got the cord. He's got the blessed cord."

Like incense in a holy place, an all-engrossing hush filled the room as Barry entered with the two-millenniums-old reliquary. With precision and care, like presenting a folded flag at a graveside, he handed the sacred box to Sister Rachel. Weeping tears of joy, not sorrow, and not wanting to defile the holy item, she immediately placed the reliquary on the mantle above the fireplace, next to the replica box made by Barry. As this startling yet tender scene unfolded, Pastor Donovan pondered, *In this living room rests the umbilical cord of Jesus, a virgin with child, ashes with our Lord's DNA, and sandwiches that were fearfully and wonderfully made. And outside this living room looms a man under arrest, an officer under suspicion, a deceived and weary world, and a congregation awaiting another homerun.*

13

"WELCOME TO THE NEW normal," expressed Ashley to Payne as they sat at the breakfast table the following Saturday. With the girls sharing stories and clothes in their bedroom and Doug still asleep in his room, the two pondered their uncommon life together. As he warmed his hands with his cup of coffee, she asked, after taking a sip of her hot tea, "Are you happy?"

"Am I what?"

"Are you *happy*?"

While Payne swallowed a few sips of coffee to stall his response, he thought, *Why is she asking me this? Do I look unhappy? Does she want me to ask her the same question? Is she projecting her own unhappiness? Is this the new normal?* Payne placed his cup down on the table and answered, "I think so. Why do you ask?"

"This morning, as I filled our tea and coffee pots, I looked out the window at the olive tree. I imagined myself doing the same thing many years from now. As I pictured the tree and the kids full-grown, I wondered, 'Will we be happy?' Payne, when we are long retired and sitting at this same table, do you think we will be happy? Will we have any regrets? Will we question our calling to be pastor and pastor's wife? Do you think our kids will loathe having been raised pastor's kids? Or will we hear, 'Well done, good and faithful parents?'"

Payne took hold of Ashley's hand and said, "Just the thought that we will still be together at this table assures me that we will be happy."

"You're bordering on sappy, Payne," said Ashley with a light chuckle and squeeze of the hand.

"I'm serious, Honey. I don't know what is in the future, but I know I want to see it with you." Then, with a smile, he said, "I do regret having been the 'pain' in your side, but I look forward to being the 'Payne' by your side as we together watch God write His story on the pages of our lives."

"You're no longer bordering Sappyville. You're walking down its Main Street."

Their shared laughter lured the girls into the kitchen. "What's so funny?" asked Anne as she poured hot water into two teacups.

"Your mother wants to defenestrate my amorous sentiments."

"Dad, as Doug would say, the magnitude of your expression is too copious for my immediate comprehension."

Perceiving that the banter bewildered Sister Rachel, Payne suggested, "Speaking of Doug, how about the two of you go wake him up? I want to have a family powwow this morning."

Payne smiled as he heard Anne explain to the sister what a powwow entailed as they left the kitchen. He kept that smile as he watched Ashley sip her tea.

* * * * *

"Where do we start?" considered Payne out loud to begin the family powwow.

"Let's start at the very beginning," voiced Doug with a hint of singing.

"A very good place to start," continued Ashley in a Maria-like voice.

"Thank you for the suggestion," said Payne with a smile. "And Honey, it's so nice to hear you sing again."

"We could be the von Donovan family," bantered Doug, "that escapes from George and SarkiSystems like the von Trapp family did from Hitler and the Nazi Party."

Payne could see that once again their wittiness bewildered Sister Rachel and that once again she gazed upon the reliquary above the fireplace as if to regain her true north. "Yes, let's start at the very beginning," submitted Payne. "Sister Rachel, we would very much like to hear about the reliquary and the blessed cord—its history and how you came to be a part of it."

With all eyes on the sister and the sister's eyes fixated on the reliquary, there in the living room, the very room where the infamous family powwow about George's plan took place, the family awaited revelation, a lifting of the veil. As if quoting a sacred text, Sister Rachel cited the holy history of the cord with watchful devotion. "Joseph and Jesus returned to Bethlehem to say 'thank you' to the innkeepers who opened up their stable. They wanted to show those gracious hosts that the baby born sixteen years ago had grown up. They also wanted to present a gift to the aging couple: a wooden box that they made together in their shop up in Nazareth. They crafted the box out of wood from the finest cedars of Lebanon. On the top they carved an olive tree with its branches draped over the sides and back, forming clever camouflage for the hinges. The tree's roots spread out over the front of the box with one root forming the sealing latch. The Nazarene carpenter and apprentice inlaid the carvings with the gold the Magi from the East presented on that most memorable visit."

After a momentary glance off the reliquary and onto her captivated audience, Sister Rachel returned her focus to the cord and its hallowed story. "When it came time for Joseph and Jesus to return home, the innkeepers proved yet again to be gracious hosts by providing food and drink for the father-Son journey. Before departing, Jesus placed His hand on the box and bestowed a blessing, a *berakah*. 'Blessed be the Lord who creates creators. Thank You for the joy of working with wood and gifting Me with a carpenter father. Preserve whatever is placed in this box. May it bring hope to Your people and glory to Your name throughout all generations.'"

Anne interjected, "I assume this box you speak of is the reliquary that SarkiSystems stole from the sisters."

"You assume correctly."

"The one here above our fireplace," clarified Doug.

"Yes."

"Cool."

"How did the box come to house the cord?" asked Ashley with her whole body leaning toward Sister Rachel.

Payne took pleasure in seeing his wife mesmerized. He did not really care if the story was history, legend, or myth. What he cared about was Ashley engaging in the story, a story he wished was myth, a dream he could wake up from, think about for a fleeting moment, and then forget about by the time he drove off to his study at church.

Sister Rachel continued, "One of the shepherds that arrived at the blessed birth placed the umbilical cord into his pouch. He protected and preserved the cord, knowing that it was the lifeline of the One who came to bring life and peace on earth. When the aged shepherd could no longer fulfill his duty, he passed the cord to his granddaughter, a trusted servant of God born in the same year as the Savior. She providentially became an apprentice to the innkeepers, learning their trade and lending her hand in the daily operations. She spent most of her free time talking and playing with the innkeepers' granddaughter. One day as they talked under a sycamore tree, she confided in her friend the existence of the cord. When Jesus and

Joseph presented the box, the girls shared the same idea: the box was made for the cord. It was the right size. Its craftsmanship befitted a holy item. And the berakah—from the very One the cord attached itself to—sealed its preservation."

Sister Rachel paused at this point, as if the story called for a *selah* moment, a time to reflect on what was just said and to prepare for what was about to be said. Her countenance indicated she was about to tread on sacred ground. "The gold-adorned cedar box and the friendship of the two girls assured the cord's continued protection. These two young ladies later followed Jesus up and down the Holy Land as He preached and presented the availability of life with God in His kingdom among us. They eventually met the blessed Mary and told her about the cord. During the tumultuous times following Jesus' crucifixion, resurrection, and ascension, they and other women disciples formed the Sisters of Saint Mary-Salome. This order, dedicated to preserving the holy umbilical cord, is the order I was destined for and the one I soon will return to."

How soon? wondered Payne. *Is she planning to fly back home right away? Is that safe to do before the baby is born? What kind of prenatal care would she and the baby receive? What kind has she received?* Prompted by this thought-process and the parting words of the doctor at the hospital, he addressed Sister Rachel with a pastor-father voice, "We need to set up an appointment with an obstetrician as soon as possible to see how you and the baby are doing."

"This is important," concurred Anne, but in a way that indicated her interest laid elsewhere. She then asked the sister, "What did you mean when you said, 'the order I was destined for'? Did you receive a calling to be a sister in the order?"

"It's more like the sisters received a calling to have me in the order," answered Sister Rachel. Her smile informed the family that she now enjoyed being the one in the know. Once again looking at the reliquary, as if for inspiration and confirmation, she shared the history, not of the cord, but of how her life was connected to the cord. "I'll start at the very beginning, because, as you say, it's a very good place to start. Sixteen years ago, early in the morning, the sisters found me outside the Church of the Nativity in Bethlehem. They found me in an apple crate, wrapped in a shawl, and wearing a secondhand t-shirt. Tucked in the swaddling shawl, near my feet, was a medallion with Saint Gabriel on it."

Payne glanced at his wife to see how she would respond to the sister's story. He understood Ashley's watery eyes because he knew her mother had dropped her off at a police station as an infant. *Will she say anything? Will she reveal this part of her story, a part that even the kids have not yet heard?*

Sister Rachel continued, "The sisters took me in, cared for me, and tried to find my parents. Nobody claimed me. There was no room for me in the nearby orphanage. So the sisters raised me. And when I was old enough, I entered their school."

"So you never met your parents?" asked Doug with bewilderment. As if disorientated, like not having a category for it, he muttered, "That sucks."

"Yes, it does," cried Ashley, "but you learn to cope and embrace that part of your story."

"Mom, are you okay?" asked Anne.

"Yes," answered Ashley with a tearful smile, "but there's something I want to share, something I have wanted to share but have not done so for one reason or another. But now I feel I have a reason. Now, I hope, is the right time." Ashley paused to look right at Payne, right at the one who knows, the one who will never leave her, the one committed to seeing her flourish. Having gathered composure and confidence, she disclosed, "Sister Rachel, I too know what it's like to not know my biological parents. I was an orphan. My mother handed me to a policeman, said, 'Here, you take her,' and then walked away. No questions asked. No shawl. No medallion. Just me in a dirty diaper. For me, however, there was room in the orphanage, and then in the foster care system."

"So how then did you meet Dad?" asked Doug.

Sensing that his son only asked this to avoid the breaking news, and himself wanting to relieve and guard his wife, Payne addressed Sister Rachel, "That's a story for another day. What I want to know is, Sister Rachel, how did you come to be here? I mean, how did you come to be involved in George's scheme?"

"A little over a year ago, sitting yet again in the schoolmaster's office, I overheard a few sisters talking about the blessed cord. That would not be unusual, for they told us students stories about it, stories about its conception and distant past. But these sisters were talking as if the blessed cord was a present reality. I heard them discussing the schedule for watching over it and which shift they were assigned to. Though walls and closed doors muffled their voices, I could distinguish one of the sister's voices and when her shift began. So, risking yet another trip to the office, I snuck out early the next morning and followed the sister, being careful not to be seen. A few minutes after she disappeared into the back of the church, and after garnering enough nerve and crafting an excuse if caught, I entered the church and made my way down a corridor, down some stairs to a chamber with an old wooden door. While admiring the door's carving, I surmised that I should just turn around, and leave. But before I could do this, the door opened and the sister being replaced, the one whose shift just ended, saw me. She ordered me to stop. She knocked on the door—a kind of code knock—and escorted me into the room to stand guilty before the sisters. As we entered, noise could be heard behind us. The sisters quickly closed the doors behind us. The sister in charge instructed me to stand directly next to the sister who caught me—and, no matter what happened, to not say one word. I watched as the sisters formed a line between a center table and the door. We heard men whispering and then a few hard knocks—not in code—sounded on the door. The head sister said a prayer, and then opened the door. Uniformed men carrying weapons entered the room. What happened next is a blur. Some things were said. The men took the reliquary from the table, and then they left. All I remember is that I was so frightened. What were the men going to do with the blessed cord? And what were the sisters going to do with me? I remained still and quiet, not out of obedience, but out of fear. I've tried to piece together what happened, but the whole ordeal paralyzed my memory."

"Would you like to know what happened?" asked Payne.

"What do you mean?" countered Sister Rachel as she took her eyes off the reliquary and looked intently at Pastor Donovan, as if searching her subconscious to see if he was there, if he was one of the armed men.

"George showed me a video of that raid." Realizing his revelation stunned the sister, he expounded, "The man leading the mission (I believe his name is Arbe) and his team had cameras attached to their bodies so that the historic event could be captured on film and used for propaganda. I confess that George used it to lure me into his plan. He approached me when my spirit and defenses were down. This is not an excuse. It's an admission that I was weak and wanting validation and ambition."

"Wanting validation and ambition—that's been the story of my life," confessed Sister Rachel. "That's why I'm here—to prove I am worth keeping. If I can return the blessed cord, then maybe the sisters will not expel me from their school. I don't want to be discarded again. I want to enter the order of the Sisters of Saint Mary-Salome. I want to be loved, and I want my child to be loved, too."

Payne opted not to comment while Ashley moved to sit right next to Sister Rachel. Following a tender moment of silence, Ashley spoke, as if declaring an edict, "You and your child are loved. Your heavenly Father and new earthly family will never forsake nor forget you."

"Will the sisters accept me 'with child'?"

"I don't know," said Ashley. "But whether or not they do, you will be blessed and a blessing."

* * * * *

"What did the doctor say?" asked Pastor Donovan to Sister Rachel and Anne as they walked out of the examining room and approached him in the waiting room. The girls' lack of response indicated that they must not have heard his question; but their smiles and conversation reassured him that the news must be good. While chauffeuring them home, he thanked God for his backseat blessings and wished that his hearing were better so he could hear what they were rejoicing about or plotting.

"Honey, we're home," announced Payne immediately upon entering the house. He motioned to the girls to join Doug and Bundt who were lounging in the living room. "Where's your mother?" asked Payne.

"She's in the kitchen," said Doug with a note of glee. "It's Taco Tuesday!" Payne and Anne joined in Doug's delight.

Anne explained to Sister Rachel, "My mom makes the best tacos. You're in for a treat."

"Let me guess, they're world famous," said Sister Rachel.

Ashley appeared from the kitchen, dressed in an apron, and holding a head of lettuce. "Dinner will be ready in ten minutes. I just need to chop the lettuce and fry the tortillas."

"Can you hold off for a moment?" asked Payne. "I want to hear how it went at the doctor's."

"I want to hear, too," said Ashley, "but can't we hear about it while we eat dinner? We don't want to rush through what the girls found out."

"And nor do we want cold meat or delayed gratification," chimed Doug. "It's Taco Tuesday! Let's eat, then talk."

"Okay, but we'll eat *and* talk," bargained Payne while his wife returned to her kitchen and the girls headed to their bedroom. For the next ten minutes, Pastor Donovan sat in his leather chair. While he savored the aroma of home cooking and gazed at the two wooden boxes resting on the mantle above the fireplace, a where-did-this-come-from conversation took place in his mind. *"What did you give up for Lent this year?" "I gave up control." "Do you find this difficult?" "Yes, especially when compared to my past fasts of giving up chips and soda." "But do you find it good?" "Absolutely, for it's helping me become the kind of person who will trust God, not force God, to do the right thing." "How do you fast from control?" "That's the difficult thing, especially when . . ."*

"Tacos are ready," broadcasted Ashley throughout the house. Payne abandoned his private conversation and followed Doug and Bundt into the kitchen with the girls filing in right behind.

"Whose turn is it to pray?" asked Doug while positioning himself to be first in line for the taco bar.

"May I pray?" asked Sister Rachel.

The whole family welcomed her unexpected request. Up to this point in her stay at the house, Pastor Donovan had not called on the sister to pray at mealtime. He did not want to presume her willingness nor force his family's faith upon her.

Bowing her head and stretching out her hands with palms up, Sister Rachel prayed, "For health and strength and daily bread, we give Thee thanks, O Lord. Amen."

Doug simultaneously picked up a plate and joined the family's collective "amen." As he methodically added chopped lettuce, shredded cheese, black olives, and salsa to his first helping of beef tacos, he said, "Dad, she can pray anytime—short, sweet, and to the point."

Once all five made it through the assembly line and were seated at the table, Payne reminded the family that they were going to hear about what the doctor had to say. His first bite into the first taco on his plate, however, reminded him of just how good the meal would be and how hard it would be to stop and talk. He would wait as they all feasted and burbled mouthfull praises, but only until they finished the first round of tacos.

"There is plenty more," said Ashley.

"No seconds until we hear from the girls," responded Payne.

"Report to us like you pray to God," said Doug with a smile and a desire for round two.

"The doctor confirmed that Sister Rachel is pregnant and beginning her second trimester," drawled Anne, speaking as slowly as possible in order to chide her brother and delay his return to the taco bar.

Sister Rachel grinned and said, "She told me that the baby is about four inches long and weighs about one ounce. Anne and I chuckled when she explained that the ultrasound would not yet be able to determine the baby's gender."

"So the visit went well," said Payne with some hesitancy, as if expecting a "however." His concern escalated with the girls' lack of immediate confirmation.

He watched them stare at each other, and then he listened as Anne spoke for both of them. "The doctor did say that something looked a bit odd, but she didn't know what. She just kept reiterating that something was peculiar about the pregnancy."

"Did you explain *how* she got pregnant?" asked Payne.

"No."

"Good."

"But the doctor did ask me if I wanted to keep it," divulged Sister Rachel.

"What?" bellowed Ashley in disgust.

"Mom, I think she asked this because she saw an unwed teenager in an exam room without the baby's father by her side. I think she wanted to give her an out. But Sister Rachel made her intentions quite clear as the visit ended."

"I told her that I will 'keep it' and that 'it' is not an 'it' but a 'he' and that she is right in thinking that there is something peculiar about my pregnancy."

"Mom and Dad, you should have seen the look on the doctor's face," recounted Anne. "We both snickered as we left the room and as we discussed the whole way home what we could have said to really confuse her and to convince her that this will in fact be an atypical and exceptional baby that she delivers this summer."

"That she delivers this summer?" inquired Ashley.

"Well, Mom, if you do the math . . ."

"I already know when, Anne. What I didn't know was where." Ashley turned to Sister Rachel and asked, "Are you planning to have your baby here?"

"Yes," replied the sister. "I guess we forgot to mention that the doctor prescribed, because of my car accident, that I rest and take it easy. She joked that I should not plan to bungee jump, but then she told me with a straight face that I was not to fly."

"I hope you know that you are welcome to stay here," said Pastor Donovan.

"I do know that. I also know that the sisters want me to come home. But I do not want to put my baby in any harm. So, yes, I do want to have my baby here. And when it is safe to fly, I want to return to the sisters with both my baby and the blessed cord."

"Sounds like a good plan," said Doug. "And you know what also sounds like a good plan? Second servings on Taco Tuesdays!"

"Well, there's plenty left," announced Ashley.

As Payne watched the others line up for round two, he remained seated and thought about the coming months. *Yes, there is plenty left, plenty of fixings lined up to spice up any life. There's George. There's Barry. There's Officer Bedford. There's the sisters. There's one, no, two more people to feed. There's Lewis Barnone, or is there? O Lord, have mercy on us.*

14

"WHERE'S THE RELIQUARY?" PASTOR Donovan panicked as he entered the front door and did not see the two wooden boxes on the fireplace mantel. For several weeks following the news that Sister Rachel and the cord would not travel back to Bethlehem, his routine consisted of coming home from work, looking at the reliquary and urn, and then saying a quiet prayer—usually expressing thanks for his growing family and for the hope they share, but often also requesting wisdom and strength to navigate through the coming months. But instead of quietly saying thanks to God or asking Him for perhaps clarity as to what and when to tell his congregation, Pastor Donovan yelled, "Where's the reliquary? The ashes? The cord? Where are they?" He needed an answer, but nobody provided one. Though he shouted, nobody responded.

Where is everybody? This initial thought opened the panic floodgates. *Did George's covert team come steal back the cord? Did they kidnap the sister? Did they kidnap everyone?* Payne scoped the living room for any evidence that would clue him as to what happened. *No sign of struggle. No forced entry.* He locked the front door and began to search the rest of the house. *Nothing unusual. Beds unmade. Clothes on the floor. And no blood!* His investigation ended in the kitchen. With the oven on and nobody cooking, Payne deduced that his wife and kids, the sister and cord were taken away in haste. Unnerved, he cried out, "Why is the oven on? Where is everybody?"

"We're out here," yelled Ashley from the backyard. "We've decided to celebrate the first day of spring by having dinner outside. The chicken and rice casserole will be ready in about fifteen minutes. Come out and see what the girls have done to the table."

Payne leaned over the sink while he regained composure. With his heart racing, he peered out the window to locate each person he moments before had believed to be kidnapped. Though all were accounted for, he remained unsettled. Following a few deep breaths to relax his tense body and anxious heart, he stepped outside and immediately asked, "Where is the reliquary?"

"It's in my closet," answered Anne. "Do you like how Sister Rachel and I decorated the table?"

"What?" Though trying hard to lay aside his anxious thoughts, he blurted, "Why did you do this?"

"To welcome spring and all that it will bring," replied Anne in defense and while placing crayons at each place setting. "The table cloth is butcher paper. During dinner, we all can write down or draw what we like about the season we are entering."

"I bet dad will list three things that start with the same letter or make up an acrostic," remarked Doug as he watered the olive tree.

"No, no," snapped Payne. "I'm not interested right now in what you did to the table. I want to know what you did to the cord. Why did you move it to your closet?"

Ashley stepped toward Payne and explained, "The girls thought that, with the temperature getting warmer, it would be better and safer to stow it away in a cooler place. I'm sorry that we did that without you knowing. It must have been a bit of a shock to not see it when you walked into the house."

Payne reached out to his wife, embraced her, and whispered in her ear, "You have no idea." Not letting her go, he continued, "I didn't think I lost just it, I thought I lost you. I never want that thought to cross my mind or heart ever again. I love you."

"Okay, you two, break it up," said Doug. "I hear the oven timer beeping. You know what that means; it's time for a little spring chicken."

"And after dinner," replied Payne, "it will be time for a little spring cleaning. Beds need to be made. Clothes need to be put away. The mantel needs dusting. The carpet . . ."

"But first we eat," interjected Ashley, "and give thanks for spring."

Everybody sat down while Anne brought out the casserole. Doug prayed a short prayer. Sister Rachel volunteered to serve the chicken and rice. Bundt sprawled next to the olive tree and chewed a tennis ball. Payne leaned back and smiled at what he observed on this first spring evening: his family home and safe, and his wife writing "Whispers from Payne" with a crayon.

* * * * *

The Cord

"It's the calm before the storm, isn't it, Dad?"

Doug's assessment disconcerted Payne as the family, including Sister Rachel, drove to church on Sunday morning. Instead of replying, Payne pretended to focus on the road when in fact he wondered, *What prompted that remark? Is Doug expecting the congregation to shun or even shame Sister Rachel? Does he think George is going to show up today for yet another surprise visit?* Unable to discern the comment or be at peace in not knowing, he asked, "What exactly do you mean by 'it's the calm before the storm'?"

"After this Sunday, the church shifts into high gear with all the activities of holy week. You'll be home after church today, enjoying the calm; but then you'll be out and about . . ."

"Enjoying the storm," interposed Payne. He has come to welcome the rhythm of holy week, the calendar of events surrounding the crux of his faith. And this year's activities added a bonus element: Pastor Donovan anticipates his full schedule providing a diversion from the past year's infamous test of his faith.

The morning's service satisfied Pastor Donovan. The people greeted Sister Rachel. He did not have to greet George. And Brother Bob said the sermon was a homerun. The rest of the day looked promising, too—a home-cooked meal, a guilt-free nap, and an evening home. Indeed, it would be the calm before the storm.

"I would like to have a powwow after I have a nap," said Payne once the family finished eating every bit of Ashley's sautéed bratwurst and green bean creation and as Ashley served up her world-famous and family-favorite "chewies" dessert.

"That's funny," said Anne, "because the sister and I were just about to ask if we could have a family meeting later today."

"Well, then, it's settled," said Payne.

"And we would like to invite Barry to join us," specified Anne.

"Why?"

"Because we have not seen him for a while. He has been so busy with school and looking for an internship. But he said he is free tonight." Payne could see uninhibited hope in his daughter when she asked, "So, can he come over later, Dad? You'd like to see him, too, right, Dad?"

"Of course" is what he said at the table, but what he thought about on the hammock in the backyard was not as assuring. *Why do the girls want to see Barry so much? Do they feel indebted to him? Is it because he is so cute? Why do they trust him? What is drawing them to him?*

The combination of the doorbell ringing and Bundt barking awakened Payne from his nap. Barry and sunset had arrived. "Let the powwow begin," broadcasted Payne to an empty backyard as he stretched and made his way inside.

"Honey, Barry is here," said Ashley as Payne entered the kitchen. Still groggy from his nap, he heard her announcement as both a warning and as a sharing in the girls' joy. He took a few deep breaths to awaken his composure and strength. He then walked into the living room holding Ashley's hand.

"Hello Barry. It's nice to see you again," said Payne. Ashley gently squeezed his hand, as if to acknowledge his candor or bluff. He wasn't sure how she perceived his performance.

"Dad, why don't you go first," said Anne. "What do you want to talk about?"

Still standing, Pastor Donovan began: "Well, as you know, I have committed myself this year to blessing others. I intend to pronounce a blessing upon each and every one of my parishioners in their homes. Along with this, I believe it would be right and good to bless God, to pronounce a blessing upon God. And, I would like to invite the congregation to join me in this spiritual exercise of blessing God and one another." Payne settled himself into his chair. From there he observed that Anne held in her lap the urn that Barry had made for her baby's ashes. He also noticed that Barry kept glancing up at the empty mantel. Payne positioned himself so that he faced Sister Rachel when he said, "I'm intrigued by the story you told about the blessed cord's early history. I'm especially interested in the blessing you referenced."

"You mean the berakah," clarified the sister, "the one Jesus pronounced upon the box."

"Yes." Pastor Donovan leaned forward in his chair, planted both his feet on the floor, and inquired, "Can you tell me more about berakahs? What are they? And how would I and my people go about writing our own?"

"The berakah is an ancient Hebrew form of prayer. God's people bless their Lord—giving thanks for who He is and for what He does. This prayer of blessing helps them notice and respond to God's blessings."

"If it's a *form* of prayer," prompted Doug, "then that means there is a formula."

Sister Rachel glanced at Anne, flashed a smile, and said, "Nothing gets passed your brother." Returning her attention to Pastor Donovan, she explained, "You begin a berakah with the words, 'Blessed be the Lord.' You then follow this phrase with a statement about a particular attribute or work of God. You conclude the prayer of blessing with a word of thanks and/or a request related to what you just expressed. Your berakah can end up being a short paragraph or a long page."

"You have experience writing this form of prayer," detected Ashley. And Payne detected warmth and affirmation in his wife's voice.

"Once a week, at school, we write our own berakah and then share it with our class. We bless—and are blessed by—one another when we do this. Communal praise strengthens and encourages faith and hope."

"Dad, sounds like something that you will want to do with the church," inserted Anne. "Now Sister Rachel and I want to talk about what we want to do with the family, and with Barry if he wants to and has the time." Anne smiled at Barry, but returned in haste to her agenda for the powwow. "This coming Tuesday, March 25, marks the one year anniversary of me becoming pregnant. Sister Rachel, when I told her this, encouraged me to commemorate this milestone in some way. So, after thinking about it, I decided that I would like to bury Joshua's ashes out by the olive tree this Tuesday night, and I would like for all of you to be with me."

Anne's words disturbed Pastor Donovan on various levels. They deflected the powwow away from his agenda; but, more troubling, they reminded him of George's agenda. *I still can't believe I fell for his plan—and that, one year later, my depraved ambition still plagues us. Will it forever be embedded in our family's DNA? Has it set into motion endless inconveniences and setbacks to be endured? Or is there a way out? God, is there a way out?*

"I think that's a great idea," offered Barry.

Cuddling the box that Barry made for her, she asked him, "Is it okay if I bury the ashes with the urn?"

"Of course."

"I have an idea," proposed Sister Rachel. "Why don't we all write a berakah and then share it on Tuesday night?"

"Are you going to grade them?" asked Doug.

"No."

"Then, why not? We sure could use a little blessing around here. And, Dad, it will give us some practice for when you invite the church to write a berakah."

Doug's verdict evidently concluded the powwow. Ashley returned to the kitchen. Doug took Bundt outside. Barry followed the girls down the hallway. Payne remained disturbed in the living room. He had no idea how to finish the sentence, "Blessed be the Lord who . . ."

* * * * *

"Barry emailed me to say that he will be able to be here tonight for the service," announced Anne as she poured milk into her cereal bowl. "He said he already wrote his berakah. He also said he could come earlier and partake of a world-famous dinner if, of course, he was invited."

"He's invited," chuckled Ashley. "And you can tell him that it's a Taco Tuesday encore."

Payne listened to this exchange with contempt for his own inability to write a simple blessing. *How come I, a seasoned pastor, can't write a berakah while Barry, a fired intern, can do so with ease?* He excused himself from the breakfast table and left for work without kissing his wife.

Tired and frustrated, Pastor Donovan sat alone in his office, unable to concentrate on Holy Week matters. Not even Taco Tuesday aroused any interest. He placed his forehead on his desk and his clasped hands on his head. With his eyes shut, he attempted to pray and break though his writer's block. So determined to have a berakah, he conned himself into forcing a blessing. But while obliging to meet this demand, God supplied an unexpected alternative—a poem that ushered Payne into a deep place of self-examination.

Take the log out

Chop

Burn

Fire of life

Guide with light

Comfort with heat

In the pit of solitude

Pastor Donovan remained still throughout this divine appointment. There would be no note taking during this mystical experience. God chiseled His message into Payne's heart of stone.

What log, Lord?

"Anger."

What? What do you mean, anger? Any anger I have pales in comparison to the anger Ashley and Anne have demonstrated. How can anger be my fault? Pastor Donovan was about to find out.

"Chop the log into smaller pieces."

Why?

"So you can see."

Like splitting a log and counting the rings, Payne's contemplative examination exposed many years of anger: sports rage as a youth, road rage as an adult, and "righteous anger" as a pastor that was not very righteous. *Look at all those rings! And look at this big ring formed this past year. Like my ladies, I have been angry with everybody. But unlike them, I have not been honest enough to express it. O God, what am I to do?*

"Release your anger into the fires of heaven. I do not want you to manage it. I want you to abhor it. Confess it. Forsake it. Burn it."

With his head still on his desk, Pastor Donovan recalled a story that a missionary shared at the church about the power of confession and repentance. While serving in the Ivory Coast, West Africa, the missionary witnessed a middle-aged man, who had trusted in fetishes his whole life, share in front of three hundred fellow villagers his faith and trust in Jesus Christ. With the pastor by his side, the man removed objects one by one from a cardboard box. He displayed each fetish for all to see, confessing the devotion and reverence he offered to them. *Chop!* One group of sticks tied together with twine was believed to bring health. Some animal hair rolled up into a ball was his hope for protection upon his crops. At the conclusion of the service, the new convert's fetishes were burned in a big public bonfire, just like in the early church when "those who practiced magic brought their books together and began burning them in the sight of all." *Burn!* Talk about firing up one's confession! This man was set free. It was time to celebrate. As Pastor Donovan recalled this story, he cried out to the Lord, *I too want to sing and dance around the fire of life.*

"First take the log out of your own eye, and *then* you will see clearly to take the speck out of your wife's and daughter's eyes."

This Sermon-on-the-Mount instruction prompted Pastor Donovan to reach out (literally) to God. Payne lifted his hands, lifted his head, opened his eyes, and prayed, *I need You to give me clarity and guidance—imputed light—as I travel this road of transformation and as I seek to help and comfort Ashley, Anne, Doug, and the rest on theirs.*

"Let us commence this blessing . . . in the pit of solitude."

For the next hour, alone in his study, Pastor Donovan wrote his berakah.

* * * * *

"Hi, Honey, I'm home," announced Payne as he entered the kitchen. While Ashley held a head of lettuce in one hand and a large knife in the other, he stepped forward, kissed her on the lips, and said with a Latin accent, "Muy sabrosa. Taco Tuesday tastes good already!"

Ashley handed him the lettuce and the knife. "And it will taste even better when it's all ready." As he began to carry out his wife-given chore, he thought he heard her say, "And it will taste even better later."

"Excuse me," said Barry, "do you have any large adhesive bandages?" His question and his presence startled Pastor Donovan. *How long has he been here? Why does he need bandages, large bandages? How many tacos will he eat?*

"Here you go," said Ashley as she handed Barry a first-aid kit. "And please tell the girls and Doug that dinner will be ready in a few minutes."

"Aren't you a bit curious as to why he needed *large* bandages?"

"I'm sure we will find out. But right now I'm more interested in where I put the black olives."

Payne found himself staring at his wife as she stretched to reach the can of olives in the cupboard and as she bent over to remove an apple pie from the oven. *Later,* sighed Payne as the two girls and two boys walked into the kitchen.

Taco Tuesday lived up to its reputation. Everybody ate seconds. And though not much conversation took place due to the preoccupation with eating, everybody complimented the chef, especially Barry, who obviously had been surviving off cafeteria and fast food and budget microwavable meals.

"I hope you all have your berakahs," said Anne. Payne heard eagerness in his daughter's voice. "Let's clear the table, rinse the dishes, put any leftovers in the refrigerator, and then meet out back for the burial."

Everybody followed these orders. With all six present in the backyard, the internment service began. Anne advanced the order of service. "We'll each read our berakah, then we'll have the burial. And then Sister Rachel and I have a surprise. So, let's have the women go first, starting with the youngest; then the men, again starting with the youngest."

Sister Rachel opened a book, a journal filled with berakahs, prayers, memories, drawings, and notes from Pastor Donovan's recent sermons. She read, "Blessed be the Lord, the God of the Sisters of Saint Mary-Salome, who has not forsaken His mercy toward this sister. He (the Good Shepherd) led me to this servant family, freed me from the deceived Deceiver, and protected the baby and me when we crashed in that underpass, that valley of the shadow of death. He has preserved the blessed cord and assured me that it, along with the baby and I, will return to its rightful guardians. May not one word fail of all His good promises as He guides me in the paths of righteousness—for His name's sake."

"Surely goodness and mercy shall follow you, Sister Rachel, all the days your life, and you will dwell in the house of the Lord forever." Doug's prophetic utterance surprised everyone, and, by the look on his face, most notably himself. "I'm sorry for speaking out of turn. Anne, it's your turn."

Anne smiled at her brother and, while holding the urn, carefully re-positioned her left hand so that she could read a seven-word berakah that she wrote on her palm: "Blessed be the Lord who restores hope." Then, with both hands tightly embracing the box, Anne spoke extemporaneously from her heart. "God sent Sister Rachel to me." Looking at the sister, she said, "You often tell me how thankful you are that God led you to me. Well, tonight I want *you* to know how thankful I am that God sent you to me. Through you He has imparted to me strength to abandon outcomes to Him. I mean, if God is for us, then who can be against us? Right, sister? You have convinced me that nothing real or virtual shall ever be able to separate us from the love of God." As if extending a hug to Sister Rachel, Anne squeezed the urn. She then continued, "Dad, I can't wait for the 'no longer any sea'—but I will because my hope in the One who is with me wherever I go has returned."

Anne paused, looking as if she might want to say more or to see if Doug had a word for his sister. When Anne indicated with a simple nod that she was done, Ashley removed a piece of paper from the pocket of her apron (an apron with "World Famous Cook" handwritten on the front). After thanking the girls for their sincerity and maturity, Ashley read her be-rakah. "Blessed be the Lord who forgives us, who releases us from the grim captivity of sin and guilt, who restores our relationships. I am addicted to His grace and committed to dispensing His grace. Because I am forgiven, I will be forgiving. So, 'Search me, O God, and know my heart; try me and know my anxious thoughts; and see if there be any hurtful way in me, and lead me in the everlasting way.'"

"I guess it's the men's turn now," said Doug after his mom placed the paper back into her apron and as he removed his fedora. He dressed up for the burial service in a suit and tie. Reading off an index card he had concealed in his hat, Doug began, "Blessed be the Lord who is a Shepherd to Sister Rachel, who restores hope to Anne, and who forgives Mom." Doug lifted his eyes from the card and said with a straight face, "Sure sounds prophetic, doesn't it? Too bad it's not what I wrote." Doug smiled, cleared his throat, and then read what he actually wrote down on the card. "Blessed be the Lord who gave me a family to live with—a mom and dad that brought me home from the hospital and kept me, and a sister that puts up with me and has not yet tried to return me." Doug stared at his card, sported a smile to mask inbound emotion, cleared his throat, and said, "That's it. Next."

Barry awaited Pastor Donovan's nod of confirmation before he began. "Blessed be the Lord who works in our lives to bring about what we do not deserve and cannot accomplish on our own. For one like me, an unemployed premed student that battles doubt and fears failure, this grace wakes me up in the morning, gets me out of bed, lifts me up as I daily stumble, and sings me to sleep at night." Though Barry finished reading, he continued, "God's grace, and the grace y'all show me, is amazing."

"Y'all?" Anne mimicked Barry as she asked, "Are you from the south?"

"Yes ma'am," replied Barry with an exaggerated drawl and smile. "But we moved away when I was ten years old when my dad's work transferred him."

"What kind of work does he do?" asked Anne and Ashley at the same time.

"He works in the aerospace business."

Silence descended upon the Donovan's backyard, as if a family pow-wow convened in a soundproof think tank. *Can SarkiSystems be considered an aerospace business? Is it possible that George is not his father? Is Barry telling us the truth? Did he say "y'all" just to throw us off? Is this the appropriate time and place to confront him? Do we risk grace?*

"Pastor Donovan, it's your turn to share your berakah." Sister Rachel's announcement broke the silence and suspended any confrontation.

Payne confessed as he unfolded the paper in his hand, "God needed to work on me before I could work on blessing Him. Let's just say, a berakah can reveal as much about the one writing it as the One being written about." With this as his introduction, he began, "Blessed be the Lord who has the best vantage point from which to judge my self-righteousness and to awaken my self-examination. He who sits on the throne of this universe can shine light into my heart so I can see just how often and easily I exaggerate the faults of others while minimizing my own. He can show me just how often and easily I inquire into the actions of others while feeding my curiosity. He can, He has, and my hope is that He will continue to direct me to take the log out of my own eye because I envision a better life, a life at peace in delegating vengeance to the One whose vision never obscures."

"Sounds like you and God had a private powwow," said Anne as she placed the wood urn into the hole that her brother dug in front of the olive tree before dinner. "Before Doug shovels the dirt back into the hole, I just want to say that this time out here together has been a blessing not just to God but to me and, dare I say, Joshua. I mean, maybe God sent him to die so that we would stand here, together, tonight, to bless the Lord. Maybe his ashes and this tree will be our reminder that hope remains, that God is with us wherever we go, even as we go to the grave, ashes to ashes and dust to dust."

Anne motioned for Doug to fill the hole, and then she invited Sister Rachel to stand by her side. "I thought about burying something with the ashes, but my sister here convinced me otherwise." Anne's abrupt statement, as well as the swiftness of the interment rite, baffled Payne. But before he could look at the puzzling speck in her eye, Anne explained, "I mentioned at the beginning that we had a surprise; and here it is." Sister Rachel held up a plastic sandwich bag with tiny pieces of something inside.

"What is it?" asked Doug. "A snack for Bundt if and when he digs up the urn?"

"No," replied Anne. "The bag contains the microchips that George implanted at the base of our necks between the shoulder blades. While you were digging the hole in the ground out here, Barry was digging out these chips. Actually, at our request, he very graciously and carefully removed the chips. Our very own doctor-in-training did an excellent job. It did not hurt too much and there was not too much blood. We then took a hammer to them and placed all the pieces into this bag. I thought maybe we should bury the crushed chips with the ashes as some kind of symbolic Freedom Act from George. But Sister Rachel said that we should simply throw the bag into the trash and have that be our final After Action Report."

Sister Rachel handed the bag to Pastor Donovan and said, "We thought, with all that these chips represent, that you would like to be the one to throw them away."

Anne thanked Barry for removing the chips and for making the urn. Sister Rachel held her stomach as she looked down at the newly covered hole and as she looked up at the plane flying overhead. Doug headed straight for the kitchen as soon as his mom reminded everyone that there was homemade pie on the kitchen counter *and* homemade ice cream in the freezer. Payne headed straight for the trashcan that would be placed out on the street and emptied in the morning. When he threw the bag into the can, he could not help but notice that it landed in a small crate filled with apple cores. He had a feeling that this might be construed as highly symbolic, but he did not want to stop and think about it. Warm, fresh pie a la mode awaited him inside, and maybe something even more luscious later!

15

SISTER RACHEL'S SECOND TRIMESTER progressed relatively quietly. Prenatal check-ups proved to be both encouraging and entertaining. Anne and she routinely met Pastor Donovan in the waiting room with smiles and muted laughter as they conveyed the doctor's analysis of the baby's development. One week the doctor said, "How did you know the baby was a boy? Was it a guess, a strong intuition? Or, with this pastor's kid as your witness, did God give you a sign?" Another week the doctor said, "The position of your baby's hands and tiny fingers makes it appear as if he's blessing us. This ultrasound printout looks almost like an icon."

Sister Rachel's second trimester coincided with the second semester of Doug's junior year of high school. Along with negotiating one bathroom with two sisters, Doug desired additional parental guidance regarding how to prepare for college. Reality sunk in when he heard friends talk about the admission exam and plans for college road trips. "Mom and Dad, what will my summer look like?" asked Doug one Saturday morning while the girls were out back watering the olive tree. "My friends will visit university campuses while I visit a hospital nursery. The baby's coming. I get that. But so is my future, and I better get ready."

Payne found himself listening a lot during this period of waiting for the baby's birth. He listened to the sisters bond. He listened to his son mature. His listened to his wife heal, even flourish. She whistled as she cooked. She engaged in conversations, both at home and at church. She beamed like a soon-to-be grandma, and he liked this sound of rebirth. He liked how God's grace drowned out the noise of past guilt and hurt and unanswered questions.

Pastor Donovan would listen to grace all day long if he could. His spirit was willing, but his flesh was too weak. But it was getting stronger. He knew he didn't deserve it, but he welcomed God's work in his life. He could see God bringing about what he as a husband, father, and pastor could not accomplish on his own. He saw grace manifested from the time he awoke to the time he fell asleep. And at the start of Sister Rachel's third trimester, he even encountered grace as he slept.

He dreamt that he visited Sister Rachel and the baby in the hospital. Both were healthy and eager to get on with life together. With feeding time at hand, Pastor Donovan said goodbye and left the hospital. Just as he was about to drive away, he saw Arbe and Dr. Greybellum enter the hospital through a side door. He thought, *Why are they here?* Then he panicked. *Is George here too? Was he released? Did he escape from incarceration? Did Barry double-cross them?*

Payne ran back into the hospital. Orange cones and caution tape blocked the elevator doors. *This is the work of George and his team*, he thought. *They've sealed off the maternity floor. They're taking the baby.* Terrified, he literally flew up the staircase, using the handrails to navigate the flight of stairs.

Entering Sister Rachel's room, he saw Arbe and Dr. Greybellum leaning over the baby. "Stand back," yelled Pastor Donovan. "Take your hands off the child and leave at once—without the baby."

"We are not here to take the baby," said Arbe calmly, unaffected by Payne's presence. "George sent us to do a DNA test to find out if indeed the baby is Jesus."

"Sit down," insisted Pastor Donovan as he seized the DNA samples from the men, "and I will tell you what you will report to George. This baby is not and cannot be Jesus. The same goes for any other baby cloned by the cord, not because the cord is not the blessed cord, but because a person is more than his or her DNA and brain chemistry. Human experience goes beyond the physical, beyond the five senses. This baby, like you and me and everybody else who has ever lived on this planet, is an embodied spirit, an unceasing spiritual being with an eternal destiny in God's great universe. Most of who he is and will become—his will, emotions, intellect, social context, character, soul—cannot be extrapolated from his DNA and grey matter, examined in a Petri dish, or transplanted into another."

"Sit down," ordered Pastor Donovan as the two men flinched to stand. "I am not done. I'll tell you when I'm done and when you can leave. Now, as I was about to say, Jesus, in His humanity, like with all human beings, was not just physical, not just an animal. You may clone sheep, but never the shepherd—and certainly not *the* Shepherd. You cannot implant *the* God gene. His infinite goodness and beauty are not locked up in neurons and synapses. His love and grace and power and justice and holiness are not found in grey matter or dark matter or any other matter. And, yet, God is more weighty and solid and real than all matter. The idea that nothing exists beyond the five senses is nonsense. The whole SarkiSystems plan is tethered to the assumptions of the scientific community's naturalism. Its systems—both the supply and the demand—are of the flesh."

Standing by the door like a royal guard, Pastor Donovan declared, "Now I am done. Now you can go, give your report, and never return."

* * * * *

"So Dad, what are you preaching on today?" asked Doug as the family and Sister Rachel settled in the car. The sister sat shotgun with her window down as they drove to church. Well into her third trimester, the July morning's cool air brought respite to her and a brisk reminder to the rest in the car that she was great with child and hot flashes.

"I'm going to paint a portrait of God."

"But Dad, you don't paint; you draw stick figures," chuckled Doug. "And stick figures do not make good portraits, especially of God."

Even with the sister's window down, Payne could hear the snickering chorus, as well as see in the rearview mirror Ashley's smiling face as she quipped, "Honey, we're not laughing with you. We're laughing at you."

Payne turned quiet, not because he was the butt of the joke, but because Doug's jibe triggered thoughts. *I may not paint, but I do preach. And what I do is significant.* Payne broke his silence with a thesis-like statement. "Although many people (though *not* you) joke about ministers and belittle the position of pastor, I think it's time to say with the Apostle Paul, 'I magnify my office,' because there is dignity to the call to be a teacher of the truth, a physician of the soul, a shepherd of God's people."

"Amen, Honey," said Ashley with a trace of guilt.

"So, what are you preaching on today?" reiterated Doug. "How are you going to paint God?"

"My text (verse three of Second John) states: 'Grace, mercy, and peace will be with us, from God the Father and from Jesus Christ, the Son of the Father, in truth and love.' I'm going to use the image of a river (symbolizing God's mercy) flowing from an abundant wellspring high above (God's grace) that supplies a beautiful lake of peace in our lives. And the banks of the stream are truth and love. Within these borders God does His transforming work. With both head and heart we . . ."

"I think my water bag just broke!" exclaimed Sister Rachel as Pastor Donovan rehearsed his sermon and as the car turned into the church parking lot.

"Are you sure?" asked Payne in a manner that conveyed, "This can't be happening—not here, not now." Admonished by Ashley's enlarged eyes glaring at him in the mirror as she leaned forward to comfort Sister Rachel, Payne recanted, "Okay, we need to get you to the hospital right away. Doug, I need you to go tell Bernard what's happening and that I will not be preaching today and that he will need to put together a praise service of songs and prayer."

Doug obeyed without hesitation. "You're sure you don't want me to preach your sermon?" inquired Doug with a smile as he leaned through Sister Rachel's open window. Payne reciprocated with a faint smirk that then morphed into a beam of pride as Doug reached in, placed his hand on Sister Rachel's shoulder, and said, "Everything will be okay. Grace, mercy, and peace will be with you in truth and love."

"Ask Brother Bob for a ride to the hospital," yelled Payne as Doug headed for the stained-glass adorned sanctuary and as his ladies and he headed for the delivery room decorated with storks carrying blue and pink bags.

* * * * *

Though tempted to ignore the speed limit, Pastor Donovan obeyed the rules of the road—partly because he wanted to keep Sister Rachel and the baby safe, but also because he did not want to attract any attention, especially the attention of the ever-looming Officer Bedford.

Helping the sister out of the car removed any doubt that her water bag had broken. "No need to worry," said Ashley in a calm but confident voice. "Anne and I will get you inside and registered while Pastor Donovan parks the car."

She's going to need a change of clothes. This car's going to need a good wash. Bernard's going to need inspiration. Doug's going to need a ride. Utility thoughts accompanied Payne to and from the parking lot. Entering the lobby and not seeing his ladies, he shouted toward the receptionist, "Where are they? Where is the girl that just came in and is about to give birth?"

The elderly lady behind the desk smiled, as if indicating that she's dealt with this scenario many times. "Your daughter just got into the elevator to go up to the maternity floor. If you want, you can fly up the stairs to meet her."

The Cord

Pastor Donovan flashed a disconcerting look, took a few deep breaths, and then stood in front of the elevator doors. While waiting, he scanned the hospital's site map hanging eye-level before him. Though having visited the hospital numerous times, Pastor Donovan never had noticed that there was a labyrinth in the courtyard. Just as the elevator doors began to open, a thought entered his mind and heart, *Go check out the labyrinth.*

"There you are," stated Ashley from the elevator. Knowing the doors would soon close, she said tersely, "They already have Sister Rachel checked in and in a room, as if they knew she was coming. Here, I'll take you to her."

As Ashley reached out to pull him in before the doors closed, Pastor Donovan reached in to stop the doors from closing. "Sounds like you have everything in control. I'll meet you up there in a few minutes. I want to go check out something here at the hospital." He withdrew his hand and donned a reassuring smile as the doors closed. As soon as he heard the elevator ascend, he headed straight for the courtyard to check out the labyrinth.

The sun dispelled the morning chill and spotlighted the plaque at the entrance to the labyrinth. Standing alone in front of a full-size replica of the labyrinth at the Chartres Cathedral in France, Pastor Donovan read the inscription on the plaque:

Ambulatio Divina

> We invite you to enter the labyrinth. It is a path to reflect in, not a maze to figure out. It is a journey to savor, not a puzzle to solve. There are no dead ends. The path will lead you to a center place and then return you to a world that God so loves.

> —The Sisters of Saint Gabriel

He stood perfectly still with his feet just outside the labyrinth. He wanted to enter, but he sensed that once he did, a divine appointment awaited him. *Do I really want to go to the center? What will I encounter on my way there? What will God say to me there?* As he prepared to venture in, he realized that if he were at church at that very moment, then he would be stepping forward to deliver his sermon. This thought undoubtedly influenced his commencement prayer: "May Your grace, mercy, and peace come to me now in grace and truth as I walk this path set before me."

Pastor Donovan's "Amen" coincided with his first step. While he steadily walked forward toward the first turn—with his head bowed, making sure to stay on the path—he heard a gentle voice say, "Whosoever wills may enter." Curiosity lifted his eyes and shifted his focus. Seeing no one, he returned to his sacred walk, his *ambulatio divina,* and pondered, *Did God just speak to me or was that my subconscious? Or, did I just trigger some audio recording the Sisters of Saint Gabriel had installed to welcome each visitor?* Unsure what to think and yet not wanting to be distracted, he simply advanced carefully along the unicursal path. Each turn seemed to evoke memorable turning points in his life, choices and events that affected him and others for better or for worse over the past year and a half. At the outset he recalled his first encounter with George at the church and then at SarkiSystems. *I was so vulnerable, so anxious to see something happen when he approached me.* More thoughts arrived as the labyrinth took Pastor Donovan in new directions. *Who am I to force God's hand? Who gave me the right to supply my daughter for an experiment? When did God start needing our counsel and meeting our demands?*

Pastor Donovan grew smaller and more naked as he progressed in the labyrinth. Guilt and confession awaited him at each switchback—not as a roadblock, but as a signpost for grace. When Ashley's car accident crossed his mind, humble gratitude moved him to pray out loud, "O God, thank You for bringing Ashley into my life and for protecting her. Forgive me when I hurt her and fail to help her flourish. Lord, please bring goodness constantly into her life and protect her; show her Your full approval and be gracious to her; smile right at her and give her peace that surpasses comprehension."

Self-examination gave voice to Pastor Donovan's thankful heart as he maintained a slow but steady pace on the labyrinth. At one point as he turned a corner and became mindful of the faith, hope, and love that he sees in his immediate and now extended family, he cried out, "I am blessed." Then, once again influenced by what would be taking place back at church, Pastor Donovan hailed, "God, You did not just hit a homerun. You hit a grand slam!"

On what turned out to be the final turn before reaching the labyrinth's center, Pastor Donovan's conversion and call to ministry emerged in his thoughts. Feelings ran deep as he prayed, "Thank You for giving me faith to believe in You, for giving me wisdom to look to You, for giving me strength to turn to You. You heard my heart's cry on that day I voiced my intention, 'I don't know what my future holds, but I know I want You to hold it.' And You know, Lord, that at that moment I had no idea You were going to call me into the ministry. But You did, and I stand amazed that my family, friends, and church affirmed Your decision. May they still do so today!" Pastor Donovan walked into the center point of the labyrinth praying, "Please increase *my* faith in Your choice. Expand my vision, build my intention, and engage me in the means necessary to be what You have called me to be."

With eyes closed and feet planted in the middle of the labyrinth's center, Payne stood perfectly still. In this sacred space he experienced freedom to let go of fixing the recent past and of controlling the immediate and ultimate future. He also experienced a vision. With his eyes shut, he saw himself fly past the moon, past the stars, and up to the very presence of God. There he stopped and heard God say, "I created you for My glory." He then responded, "For Your glory, Lord, I live." He then returned. Pastor Donovan opened his eyes to find that indeed he was standing in the center of the labyrinth. Closing his eyes, he found himself again flying past the moon. But this time, he looked to his right and saw Ashley and Doug, Anne and Joshua, Sister Rachel and her baby, Barry and the sisters coming with him past the moon, past the stars, and up to the very presence of God. There they all stopped and heard God say, "I created you for My glory." To which they responded in unison, "For Your glory, Lord, we live." Again, Pastor Donovan opened his eyes; again, he found himself in the center of the labyrinth. Closing his eyes one more time, he immediately became aware that the trip he just experienced was not a journey up and out, but rather one deep within. In the center point of his life, in his very soul, he heard God say, "I created you for My glory." And from this same place he heard himself say, "For Your glory, Lord, I and we live."

Pastor Donovan opened his eyes, looked up and noticed that the sun's position denoted it was getting late into the eleventh hour. Time had come to return to the world that God so loved. He felt himself growing bigger and being clothed in righteousness as he followed the path back out. As he walked, he blessed the Lord and those fellow travelers in his vision. And as he walked out from the labyrinth and toward the elevator, he sang, "O that with yonder sacred throng we at His feet may fall! We'll join the everlasting song, and crown Him Lord of all; we'll join the everlasting song, and crown Him Lord of all!"

* * * * *

"Where have you been?" asked Anne as she held Sister Rachel's hand and as Ashley stood on the other side of the bed tracking the time between contractions.

"I was out in the courtyard getting fresh air and checking out the labyrinth."

"The what?" asked Anne.

"They have a labyrinth here?" asked the sister with an exhausted yet elated smile.

"You know what a labyrinth is?" asked Anne.

"Yes, we have one at our school," answered the sister. "It is a way to . . ." An intense contraction interrupted her description, as did the subsequent series of deep breaths.

The pangs of childbirth moved Pastor Donovan away from the bed and up against the far wall. To distract his uneasiness, he opened the blinds and looked out the window. Serendipitously, down below, in plain sight, stood the labyrinth. "Anne," beckoned Payne rather spiritedly, "come here and I will show you what a labyrinth looks like." From the delivery room three stories above the courtyard, he explained the gist of the labyrinth to his daughter. Then, as he was about to share what happened on his sacred walk, two things occurred. Anne heard Sister Rachel's next contraction and thus returned to comfort her. And secondly, he saw Doug wandering through the courtyard, as if lost and looking for the elevator. *He must have taken a wrong turn when Brother Bob dropped him off.* While thinking this, Pastor Donovan observed his son stopping at the entrance of the labyrinth—and then entering. As he watched Doug traverse his way along the path, he became oblivious to the affairs in the room. Standing still with his head bowed, he stared out the window and wondered, *What is Doug experiencing right now? Where is the labyrinth taking him? Did he hear, "Whosoever wills may enter"?*

At some point while gazing down at his son's *ambulatio divina*, Pastor Donovan's own labyrinth experience reconvened. From his new third-story perspective, he perceived the labyrinth to be multidimensional. It appeared before him as an enormous, multilayered, interlocking timepiece. He saw individual labyrinths on distinct levels, fitting together, and working together. All the parts were moving and quickly converging and forming into a single unit, as if being guided to a final goal.

While still looking out the window, a window that now looked out upon the grand story of humankind, Pastor Donovan saw both the remarkable and mundane carry purpose. He witnessed seemingly insignificant events like the oboe player visiting the church and the preparation of world-famous meals playing a part in and adding weight to the operation of the whole. He watched them link with and fit into noteworthy events like the birth of Jesus Christ and the death of Joshua Donovan. The blessed cord and the olive tree dovetailed together in the great timepiece of history where all the pieces were working pieces. And the consummation of this operation was at hand. Pastor Donovan heard a thunderous voice, "It's time." He stood in awe as he anticipated the imminent and climactic completion of the grand plan. With great anticipation he imagined what would happen when the final piece fit into place.

Again the voice thundered, "It's time. He's coming."

Unspeakable joy filled Pastor Donovan's whole being when he heard this. He cried out, "Amen. Come, Lord Jesus!"

"Payne, it's time. He's coming. Honey, don't just stand there, the baby's coming."

* 9 7 8 1 4 9 8 2 2 9 6 3 0 *